Hunter Enslaved

Tarron Hunters: Book 2

NOLA ROBERTSON

ISBN-13:   978-0-9981511-7-5

CHAPTER ONE

"Oh shit." Hank, one of the night shift miners, jumped out of his chair and nearly collided with Libby. She managed to swerve out of his way without spilling the last drink on her tray.

Shaking her head, she walked around one of the three occupied tables at the Nexus. She set a tall glass of ale imported from Earth in front of another miner, then glanced at the long translucent gray bar on the opposite side of the room.

Hank fisted a handful of his drunk friend's shirt and hauled him off the counter. After saying something to Ricka, the bartender and her roommate, he helped Jimmy stagger to the door. He'd almost made it out of the building when Jimmy swayed to the left and banged his head against the synthetic metal frame. The thud was so loud, Libby winced.

Her heart went out to the poor guy. Other than a handful of families, the colony was predominantly populated by men. The majority of them worked for the mining corporation. Excavating and supplying the dryterron ore to other planets was Rivean's main source of business.

Poor Jimmy hadn't even been on the planet six months before the lonely existence got to him. She'd seen him drink excessively night after night until he worked up the courage to propose to Ricka.

She understood better than most the loneliness he felt. She'd arrived on the planet via the colony's bride program, filled with the promise of a better future. Within months of her marriage, she'd lost

1

her husband in a freak mining accident. Trey had always been good to her. She hadn't loved him, not in the way a man and woman committed to each other should. He'd been her best friend, and she'd cared a great deal for him. Given time, she'd believed she might have fallen in love with him.

It wasn't as if she didn't get any offers. She did, plenty of them. Avoiding another relationship had been by choice. Most of the men here weren't interested in anything substantial. They wanted someone to share their bed until their three-year contract with the mining corporation terminated and they returned to Earth.

A slap on her left butt cheek startled her, and she spun around. Carl flashed crooked teeth through his wide grin. Unlike the rest of the miners, he hadn't bothered to remove his work coveralls before coming to the bar. Flecks of yellow ore clung to the blue fabric and speckled his stringy hair. He smugly grabbed for her again. "Hey, baby. Why don't you come home with me tonight?"

So not going to happen. Glowering, she quickly moved out of his reach. She curled her fingers around the rim of the tray, and fought the impulse to tell him to go screw himself. Aware of his obsession with her backside, she'd gotten good at avoiding his roaming hands. She silently cursed herself for being so preoccupied, she'd forgotten to stay clear of the table.

His buddy, Boyd, leered at her and chuckled, irritating her even more. The man towered a good six inches over the other miners in the room. Everything about him, from his manicured nails to the designer clothes imported from Earth, spoke of wealth and power. Not a single strand of his chestnut-colored hair was ever out of place. Heck, he probably used more hair products in a week than she could afford in a year.

She avoided him more than she did Carl. She'd heard rumors that he'd roughed up a girl or two at the pleasure house a few blocks away. Whether it was true or not, she had no idea. There was just something sinister in the way he looked at her, and it majorly creeped her out.

The asshole was the nephew of Dale Keagan, the mining company's owner. The last thing she wanted, or needed, was a problem with either one of them. The elder Keagan pretty much ran the planet, and had the power to make her life hell. It was the only reason she continued to put up with the constant ogling and ass grabbing from the two men.

She'd hoped if they'd heard the word "no" often enough they'd finally get the message and lose interest. No such luck. If anything, her negative responses seemed to encourage their persistence.

Boyd licked his lips. "Maybe she'd prefer a real man between her legs."

Carl flipped him off. "Fuck you, Keagan."

Can he be any more of an asshole? Libby could feel the heat rising on her cheeks. It had already been a long week, and she didn't need any more of their crap. She wished to heck that everyone would leave, especially these two, so they could close up and go home.

Ignoring the men's grating laughter, she headed for the bar. After setting the serving tray on the counter, she slid onto one of the empty stools across from Ricka. "I know we need the tips to get off this forsaken planet, but if the new guy on Marty's crew smacks my ass one more time, I swear I'm going to hit him over the head with my tray." She scowled at the jerk over her shoulder.

Ricka smiled, picked up a discarded glass, then swiped a damp cloth over the counter. "You want me to talk to him?"

Libby appreciated that her friend was always willing to stand up for her, but at tempting as it sounded, she wasn't willing to have Ricka end up on Keagan's radar either. "No. They're done ordering, and I'll wait until they leave to clear away the glasses." Libby tapped the counter. "I almost forgot. The guy in the back wants another dreva."

"Damn, that's his third one tonight. I'm surprised he hasn't toppled over yet."

Libby was thinking the same thing. She'd seen some big guys, capable of holding large quantities of liquor, drop to their knees after a few sips of the potent drink.

Ricka turned toward the mirrored wall behind her and snatched a tall square black bottle off the shelf. After pouring the dark blue liquid into a tall glass, she set it on the serving tray.

"I know. It doesn't seem to bother him." Libby shrugged and tucked a loose blonde curl behind her ear. "Maybe he comes from a planet where they have a higher tolerance."

"Yeah, maybe." Ricka glanced at the man.

Libby leaned on the counter and lowered her voice. "Well,

wherever he's from, they sure know how to put a guy together in all the right places. And those unusual eyes, they're so…"

"Intoxicating," Ricka finished.

"So you have been looking." Libby could definitely see the man's appeal. He was impressively large, and his dark hair draped across a set of broad shoulders. His blue-green eyes were catlike, and he had interesting black markings starting along the left side of his neck and disappearing beneath the collar of his shirt.

"I might be avoiding men at the moment, but it doesn't mean I don't take notice when someone so amazingly attractive comes in here," Ricka said.

Libby glimpsed over her shoulder. "There's definitely some interest there. He hasn't stopped staring at you since he got here.

"I say you go for it. He's an off-worlder, so technically you wouldn't be breaking any of your rules. One night with him and you'd probably be good for another year. And you got your shots last month, so you don't have to worry about picking up any strange diseases or getting an unwanted surprise in nine months." The colony had a strict "no children unless authorized" policy, and getting the mandatory annual birth control injections was heavily enforced. All women, including those who didn't work for the pleasure houses— the colony's way of helping the miners cope— were required to get the shot.

"Heck, I might even be tempted to go for it myself if he showed me any interest," Libby teased. She worried about Ricka. Her friend hadn't gotten involved with a man in over a year, not since her father's death. She'd lost her home, courtesy of some stupid rule implemented by the colony. Since Libby had dealt with the same problem the previous year, she'd invited her to share her living unit, then helped her get the bartending job. Not a great place to work, but it sure beat the heck out of the prospect of being a pleasure worker.

Shortly afterward, they'd devised a pact to purchase a one-way flight on a ship bound for Earth. The darned things were extremely expensive, and it was taking longer than they'd hoped to save up the necessary funds. It was almost as if the Keagans wanted to keep the women from leaving the planet.

"Jeez. Stop already." Ricka laughed and snapped the cloth at her. "I appreciate you intervening on behalf of my sex life, but I'm good."

"Sure you are."

The heavy wooden door at the front of the building banged against the wall. Libby jumped, nearly falling off her seat. A Klorthon stood in the doorway, a warrior breed of alien and one she knew was meaner than hell.

She hated staring, but she couldn't help it. These guys terrified the crap out of her. It was a good thing the Rivean mining colony didn't have anything interesting to draw the breed to the planet, or who knew how many of them would be visiting on a regular basis.

From what she'd overheard from the miners, those who did land usually ended up in one of the pleasure houses. The last time the warriors had found their way to the bar, they'd arrived in a group. This one was alone, so maybe it wouldn't be so bad.

The few she'd seen, and thankfully it wasn't many, all had the same pale orange skin stretching across overly defined cheekbones and pointed chins. This guy had long shoulder-length hair a dull bleached-out shade of white. He was nothing close to handsome, more like scary. Old-horror-movie scary, like the ones she viewed on the virtuals she'd brought with her from Earth.

Clothed in a light-brown leather vest across a set of huge abs, his leather pants barely constrained long thick-muscled legs making him appear massive and intimidating. Libby slowly eased off her stool wishing she was on the other side of the counter with Ricka.

Orum, the bar's owner, had been sitting at the far end of the bar nursing a drink most of the night. He widened his eyes and clutched the glass. The warrior hadn't taken more than two steps before their boss slid his overweight body off his stool. He ducked down the hallway leading to the back of the building, more than likely looking for a place to hide. Libby frowned. She couldn't believe the jerk had deserted them.

She noticed the guys sitting at the table closest to the door move to the edge of their seats, no doubt getting ready to make a hasty exit. The warrior strode toward the counter. He barely noticed her, his attention focused on Ricka.

"Why don't you take care of your customer? I've got this," Ricka said.

"Are you sure?" Libby picked up her tray.

"Yeah. Now go."

5

Nodding, she hastened toward the back of the bar. She hated leaving Ricka alone but knew her friend was a lot tougher and better equipped to deal with the warrior than she was. "Here you go." She set the glass of dreva in front of the stranger, nearly spilling the contents because her hand was shaking.

She clutched the tray securely to her chest, her attention focused on what was happening at the bar. The room had grown eerily quiet, everyone focused on the Klorthon as he straddled one of the stools and propped his elbows on the counter.

Libby might be too far away to hear clearly, but she got a good view of the man swiping his long dark-purple tongue across his lower lip, and could guess what the conversation was about. Her stomach roiled with repulsion. How was Ricka able to handle being so close to him?

Apparently, whatever Ricka said after the warrior slapped something on the counter must have pissed him off. He grabbed her wrist and yanked her forward, slamming her against the edge of the counter. Ricka inched her right hand behind her back. *Crap, she's going to get herself killed.* Libby wanted to scream, throw her tray, do something to stop her friend from reaching for the knife she knew was hidden under her shirt. She hated feeling helpless, but there wasn't anything someone her size could do against a man who was built like a wall and stood well over six feet.

Ricka yanked out the knife and pressed it against the warrior's neck. "I said, get your hands off me." There was no mistaking her angry words.

"You think to threaten me with this tiny piece of metal?" the warrior asked.

"It's not a threat. You can let go of my arm or bleed out on the floor after I slice your throat. Your choice."

None of the miners were armed, and probably wouldn't help if they were. Ricka kept a weapon hidden under the bar, but neither one of them was close enough to reach it. Desperate to help her friend, Libby turned to the stranger sitting next to her. "Do something, please."

He got to his feet, the chair falling backward onto the floor. Flipping aside his long jacket, he withdrew a laser repeater from the holster on his hip. "I would do as she asks."

The Klorthon jerked his head in their direction. He bared his teeth and made a noise similar to a growl. The two men glared at each other for what seemed like forever before the warrior released Ricka. He threw back his head and laughed. "My apologies. I did not mean to offend."

Ricka backed away from the bar and rubbed her wrist. By the way she glared at the warrior, Libby didn't think her friend believed his empty words any more than she did. Too afraid to move, Libby stood off to the side and watched the stranger return to his seat. He trained his intense gaze on the Klorthon.

The warrior slapped the counter. "Pour me a tall ale."

"Sure." Ricka grabbed a bottle and glass, then poured a drink and set it on the edge of the bar.

After downing the amber liquid in a single swallow, he smacked the glass on the counter and slid off the stool. Reaching into his pocket, he tossed some coins in her direction. "I will do as you suggest and seek my pleasure elsewhere." He picked up whatever he'd dropped on the counter earlier and headed for the exit.

Libby rushed behind the bar, tossed the tray aside, and pulled Ricka into a hug. "Are you okay?"

"I'm fine."

Libby didn't think she was fine, not by the way her fingers gripped the edge of the counter.

Marty, one of the older miners who always looked out for them, walked up behind them. Worry etched his graying temples. "Damn, kiddo. When I bought you the knife, I never thought you'd try to take on a warrior with it."

"He's right," Libby scolded. "What were you thinking? That was either the stupidest or the bravest thing I've ever seen you do."

"Definitely not one of my smarter moves." Ricka grabbed a clean glass and another bottle, then poured a drink, spilling some of the liquid over the rim. She tipped back her head and drained the shot.

"It's a good thing the Tarron was here," Marty said.

"Tarron? You mean the guy is a hunter?" Ricka asked.

"Yep. Quadrant enforcement. They tend to stay clear of us since the patrol polices the colony. I've only seen a few of them over the years. Real tough bastards. Only someone with a death wish would mess with one." He patted her shoulder. "You still look pale. You gonna be okay? We have another long shift tonight, and I need to get these young pups home, but I'll stay if you need me."

"I'm good."

"If you're sure," Marty said.

"Positive. Now go. Stop hovering."

Libby waited until the group of miners left. "Do you think he'll be back?"

"I'm sure he's already found someone to keep him busy for the night." Ricka tipped her head and looked over Libby's shoulder. "As long as the hunter is here, we shouldn't have anything to worry about."

Libby took a deep breath, trying to relax. "I guess you're right."

"Why don't you let the other table know its last call for drinks, and I'll start cleaning up."

As far as a night of work went, the evening's events ranked right up there on the top ten of Libby's never-want-to-repeat scale. Never. Ever. Again.

She was still a little shaky from watching Ricka be accosted by the Klorthon. Now that the hunter and the late night-shift miners had gone, her tables were cleaned, the bar was closed, and all she wanted to do was go home. "You about ready to go?" Libby set her belongings on one of the stools and propped her elbows on the translucent gray counter.

Ricka tucked a strand of dark auburn hair behind her ear, then washed the last of the dirty glasses and set it on the rack under the sink. "Let me get my things." She opened the cabinet behind the bar and retrieved a travel pouch and jacket.

"Where's Orum? I didn't see him cowering in his office," Libby said.

"He left about five minutes ago, grumbling about needing to be somewhere, and said to lock up."

"Fine by me. The less I have to deal with him, the better." Libby tugged on her coat and headed for the exit.

"Totally in agreement with you there."

Once they were outside, Ricka secured the door and keyed in the lock sequence. Even with the coat, the chilly air made Libby shiver. The planet had a dry atmosphere, comparable to the desert areas on Earth, only hotter. While some of the days could be real scorchers, the evenings tended to be cooler, sometimes frigid.

They headed for the narrow alleyway leading to the lot behind the building where Ricka kept her transport parked. "Is it me, or is the walkway darker than normal?" Libby asked.

"Damn, the solars are out again. And not only the ones on our building—they're out on the supply store next door too." The solars went out all the time. No matter how much they complained to Orum—and they complained a lot—their cheap boss wouldn't invest in any decent lighting.

Ricka snagged her sleeve. "I don't like it. Maybe we should go around."

By around, she meant two blocks out of the way. Sure there would be more light and possibly a colony patrol vehicle making rounds, but it would take them longer to reach the lot. "It's freezing, and I'm exhausted," Libby whined, trying to disguise the real reason she wanted to get to the transport as fast as possible. She was afraid the Klorthon might still be lurking around and she didn't want to waste any time getting safely locked inside the vehicle.

"I still think we should…" Ricka said.

Libby didn't give her a chance to change her mind. "Come on, it's not far." She quickened her pace and headed for the lot. "There's still enough light to see where we're going. It won't take long if we hurry."

"Wait for me," Ricka hollered, taking no more than a couple of seconds to catch up with her.

The passageway filled with the echo of heavy footsteps. Footsteps that didn't belong to either of them. Libby stopped, her heartbeat hammering in her ears. "Did you hear something?"

"Yeah." Ricka peered behind them. "Keep moving. We're almost there." Libby didn't resist when she grabbed her hand and pulled her forward, urging her to move faster.

They hadn't made it far when the Klorthon from the bar appeared in front of them, his massive frame blocking their path. He took a menacing step forward. "Did you miss me, female?"

She gasped and gripped Ricka's hand tighter. "Oh my God. I'm so sorry. I should have listened to you."

Ricka took a protective step in front of her, but not enough to block her view of the warrior. "What do you want?"

"You and I have unfinished business," he said.

"I told you before, I'm not interested."

"I like your spirit and will take great pleasure in breaking it."

Ricka lowered her voice, barely above a whisper. "No matter what happens, you run when I tell you." She spoke louder to the warrior. "Like I said, still not interested."

Irritation burned in his arrogant gaze. "I will have you. Make no mistake."

"The only mistake I made was not slicing your throat when I had the chance."

Libby tugged on her sleeve. "What are you doing? Are you nuts?" There were times she envied Ricka's courageous attitude. Now was not one of them because if she wasn't careful she was going to get them both killed.

"Be ready."

No, no, no. She's going to do something stupid. Again.

Ricka straightened her shoulders and didn't budge when he stalked toward her. As soon as he seized her arm, she jerked her knee upward and nailed him hard in the groin. A roar ripped from his throat. He shot her a murderous look and gripped his crotch before dropping to the ground.

"Run!" Ricka shouted.

Without hesitation, Libby spun around and ran toward the front of the building. *Crap.* If the warrior managed to catch them now, they were definitely going to die. She'd barely made it ten feet when a transport stopped in front of her, blocking their exit. The door slid open and another Klorthon jumped out. Before she could get away, he seized her around the waist.

"Let me go!" she screamed.

"Silence," He growled and clamped a strong hand roughly over her mouth.

Libby frantically clawed at his wrists and kicked his legs. Neither seemed to phase the warrior as he hoisted her off the ground and carried her to the rear of the vehicle. He tossed her into the cargo area.

Libby groaned when she connected with the hard floor, the pain jolting her knees and radiating along her legs. She scrambled to her feet, but before she could get out he slammed the door shut, leaving her in darkness. "Let me out," she yelled and pounded on the thick metal door until her hands throbbed.

Several minutes later, the transport lurched forward, the momentum forcing her to drop to her knees again. With unsteady hands, she felt her way around the confining enclosure until she found something to lean her back against. She wrapped her arms around her legs, pulling them tight against her chest. What had happened to Ricka? All she could think about were the terrible things the Klorthon said he had planned for her friend. Was he following through on his threat? Or had the warrior already killed her? Was that why they hadn't thrown her in the back of the vehicle too?

She'd heard stories about women being abducted and sold into slavery. Human females were highly coveted because they were compatible breeders to many of the species in this quadrant. Was that what she had to look forward to? Being sold to some wealthy buyer, her body used repeatedly for someone's sick pleasures.

If only she'd listened to Ricka and stayed out of that damned passageway, maybe they'd both be at home. Safe.

Overcome by the hopelessness of her situation, she dropped her forehead to her knees, no longer able to stop the tears from falling.

#

Erak Dakros sat on the edge of the narrow bed in his quarters aboard the midsized hunter space vessel. The last few weeks had been excruciatingly painful, not physically, but emotionally. He was glad to be returning to his home on Tarron. He finished tugging on one of his boots, then reached for the beeping communication device attached to the black belt of his uniform. "Yes." He pressed the button to activate an intership link.

"Command is requesting to speak with you," Larn, one of the other two hunters on the ship, answered. Erak could hear the irritation in his low, gravelly voice.

"On my way." Erak sighed and disconnected the link, then pulled on his other boot. He got to his feet and strapped on the holster containing his repeater. An attack on their ship in this quadrant was highly unlikely, but he always liked to be prepared.

He didn't believe the call was routine, especially since his last report to command had occurred less than a day ago. Reluctantly, he headed for the control room located at the opposite end of the ship.

They'd recently completed their mission to safely deliver the daughter of an emissary who'd been visiting his planet back to her family on Ryserna. In public, she might be attractive and charming, but once she'd boarded his ship, the spoiled and arrogant female had turned into a demanding shrew, though the more popular term his men preferred was bitch.

It seemed like the torturous trip had lasted for months. In reality, it had only been a little more than a week, but even that was enough to deplete the last of his patience. He knew the other two men's tolerance levels hadn't fared much better. He'd had to listen to their daily complaints, both during and after the assignment had finished. Balok, the other team member, excelled at negativity and grumbled the worst.

Erak despised these types of missions. Enlisting with the hunters had been his way of escaping from the political environment he'd been raised in. Yet, somehow, being the son of prominent diplomats always put him at the top of Commander Ryos Davenger's list when it came to being given this kind of assignment.

When he reached the control room, he found both men in attendance. Balok sat in the copilot seat next to Larn.

"Surely the commander is not going to send us on another mission. We deserve a few days off and an increase in pay for having to deal with all those tantrums," Balok said as soon as Erak entered the room.

"I still cannot believe someone so attractive could be so mean-spirited." Larn rubbed the nearly healed bruise on his forehead and stepped away from the pilot's chair. "Or aim so well."

"I cannot believe you did not learn to duck better." Erak took the seat Larn had vacated. He tapped a key on the panel, and an image of the commander, scowling more than usual, appeared on the virtucom screen. Whatever Ryos had to say must be important. The man very rarely issued instructions in person, usually leaving the task to one of several junior officers. "Sir." Erak knew his boss preferred to forgo formalities and get straight to business.

"I know you and your team deserve a much-needed break, but a grave situation has arisen," Ryos said.

Erak hoped the issue didn't involve another diplomat or their overindulged offspring. Another week of listening to Balok's protests, and he might be tempted to remove his repeater and shoot him.

"As you are aware, we have spent years unsuccessfully trying to locate the whereabouts of the slavers. We recently received a report that three females were abducted from the colony on Rivean. Synge was in the area and confirmed it was a group of Klorthons led by Molock."

Erak knew his friend Synge had always suspected the warrior was somehow involved with the numerous female disappearances reported in this area. After all this time, they still had no idea who the slavers were or how they'd managed to elude detection. For his friend to have confirmation was a much-needed breakthrough.

"He prevented the kidnapping of a fourth female and is bringing her to Tarron. The colony patrol has tracked the location of the Klorthons. They have requested our assistance in intercepting their vessel. Your ship is the closest we have in the area."

"If the patrol knows their ship's location, why do they not apprehend them?" Larn asked.

"Dale Keagan, the head of the mining corporation, controls the operations on the colony. He refuses to allow the patrol to openly get involved because it could jeopardize the large amount of business they have with Klorthon," Ryos said.

The information didn't surprise Erak. He'd never met the owner of the Rivean-based company, but he'd heard plenty of stories about the man's ruthless and greedy reputation. Risking his resources or the lives of his employees to save the women would mean nothing to him unless there was a profit to be made from it.

"I am sending you the information on the females who were taken, along with the coordinates for the Klorthon's vessel." Ryos tapped his fingers on the panel in front of him.

Several seconds later, the data arrived on a separate control display. Erak studied the images of the three females, his attention drawn to the human named Libby Evans. *Blonde hair and blue eyes.* Her appearance was very appealing, and he could understand why she'd been taken. The hair color alone was a rare commodity and would be highly valuable. He turned his attention back to Ryos. "What are your orders?"

"At this point, we have no idea how large the vessel is, or how many warriors are in the crew. Proceed with extreme caution. Do not engage unless you can do so without endangering yourselves or the females. Ultimately, we cannot allow them to be turned over to the slavers."

"And if we encounter the slavers?" Larn asked.

"Again, do not engage."

"But, sir, we could…" Balok argued.

"No. As much as I want to find the head of their organization, I will not risk lives to do so. I am sending another team, but it will take time for them to reach your location."

"Understood," Erak said. The identity of the slavers had eluded them for quite some time. Putting an end to the abductions was at the top of every hunter's list. To be this close and be ordered to do nothing was frustrating.

"I expect a report as soon as you have any information." Ryos disconnected the link, and the screen faded to black.

"Are we really going to sit back and do nothing if we find them?" Larn asked.

Erak noticed Balok's equally annoyed expression. "We will follow orders." He wanted to prevent any other females from being taken as badly as they did, but he did not intend to put their lives at risk. Hopefully, the additional support the commander had sent would arrive in time to assist them.

"Lock in on these coordinates and let me know as soon as something is detected by the tracker." He leaned back in his chair and rubbed the tension tightening his neck, then waited for the grumbling to begin.

"We have a problem." Balok ran his hand over the panel, tapping numerous buttons with his fingertips. "The controls are no longer responding. Even the trackers have been jammed."

An alarm ripped through the room. *Fuck. We are being breached.* Erak jumped to his feet and drew his repeater.

CHAPTER TWO

Libby had no idea how much time had passed since she'd been locked away in the cargo bay on the Klorthon's ship. The uncomfortable transport ride on Rivean had ended somewhere in a secluded area away from the city. From there, she'd been hustled onto a shuttle with two other women and transferred to a much larger ship somewhere in space.

If she had to guess, this was not the first time the modified storage area had been used to transport prisoners. There were ten cots, five on each side of the room, with a portion of the frame bolted to the thick metal walls. In one corner, a small stall had been fashioned into a bathroom. Not necessarily clean or comfortable, but it served its purpose and disposed of waste.

She sat on the edge of one of the beds wondering what had happened to her friend. Ricka was tough and resourceful. No way would she let the Klorthon get the better of her. She'd probably found a way to escape and was hopefully searching for her.

After being tossed into this room, she'd learned the other women had also been abducted from the colony. Britta, another human with mousy brown hair, sat on one of the cots with her back braced against the wall. She was barely twenty-two years old and had recently arrived on the mining colony, also via the bride program. Apparently, she'd been unaware of the dangers venturing around the city alone after dark posed and had been easy prey for the Klorthons.

The other woman, Kala, casually paced the floor. Her strapped burgundy heels clicked loudly against the metal. She was a

Rhylarian, a species schooled in the art of sexually pleasing a man, and worked for the colony at one of the pleasure houses. Dark layered hair and heavy makeup enhanced her ash-gray skin. Inspecting her tall, well-muscled body and full lips tinted a deep shade of plum, Libby could easily see her appeal to the miners.

She'd met Kala before, having served her and her coworkers a few times at the bar. After a recent conversation, Libby had learned that not much bothered her. Evidently, the Rhylarians were an emotionless race, viewing the world logically. It was probably why they were successful in the pleasure business. According to Kala, they were able to work without developing an attachment to their clientele.

Britta sniffled and swiped at the puffy skin below her reddened eyes. "Do you have any idea where they're taking us?"

Kala waved her hand nonchalantly through the air. "My guess is we are going to be sold to slavers. They probably have some wealthy buyer who's too fat and hideous to get a woman on his own."

Britta cringed, and a fresh bout of tears streamed down her cheeks. "You, you don't really believe that, do you?"

"Believe me, being sold is preferable to remaining on board this ship. Klorthons view women as nothing more than a possession, to be used, then traded to another. Some of them can be very rough and abusive."

Libby had already come to the same conclusion regarding their fate. For Britta's sake, she wished Kala wouldn't be quite so descriptive or blunt with her explanations. The younger woman appeared fragile and close to snapping.

Britta shook her head in denial. "This can't be happening. Poor Donny will come home, and I won't be there. We had a fight before he left for work. Now he's going to think I left him."

Libby got up and went to sit next to her. "I'm sure your husband won't think you deserted him."

"He still won't know what happened to me." Britta's voice quivered, and she sniffled some more. "No one is going to look for us, are they?"

"I'm sure someone will have reported our disappearances to the patrol, and they'll send someone to find us." Libby didn't believe the reassuring words but hated to see Britta so upset.

Kala snorted. "I fear your beliefs are incorrect. No one..." The sound of the metal door sliding open drowned out her words.

Two warriors Libby had never seen before strode through the entryway, supporting another man between them. His deeply tanned skin was a rich contrast in comparison to the pale orange of the Klorthons. His head hung forward, and long strands of golden-brown hair covered his face. He wore skintight black pants and dark boots, but his bare, thick-muscled, and broad chest was covered with bruises and cuts.

As soon a she saw the black markings running along his left shoulder and the side of his chest, she knew he was a hunter. The second one she'd ever seen. What was he doing here and why had they beaten him? Was it possible he'd been sent to find them and had somehow ended up a prisoner?

"Please don't let them take me," Britta whimpered and scooted next to her.

"It'll be okay. Stay here and be quiet." Libby patted the hand clinging to her arm.

The warriors dragged the man farther into the room, then shoved him forward. He staggered a few steps, and dropped to the floor with a grunt. Kala looked at the man on the floor, then back to the warriors, her impassive expression never changing. Britta screamed and jerked her legs up onto the cot as if a snake had been tossed at her feet. *What part of stay quiet didn't she understand?* Libby glanced at the warriors, relieved to see they were ignoring her outburst.

One of the men tossed a red shirt next to the fallen man's feet. "You should be glad you are so pretty. Molock has a female buyer who is willing to pay quite a bit for a new breeder."

The other Klorthon laughed. "It is a much better fate than that of your friends. They were sent to the fighting arenas. I hear no one lasts in the fights longer than a month. Once the crowd grows tired of them, they are tossed out the airlock. Not a pleasant way to die." His humor faded when his gaze landed on Libby. "What do we have here?" He licked his lips. "I have never had a human female before."

After her stomach's reaction the last time, Libby had hoped she'd never have to see another one of those disgusting purple tongues again. To make the bout of nausea worse, his silver orbs darkened with lust.

The other warrior grabbed his arm. "You heard Molock's orders. He will kill anyone who touches the females. Our buyer will arrive soon, and he will not pay for damaged merchandise."

He yanked his arm free. "I promise not to leave a mark."

This can't be happening. Libby's mouth went dry, and she tried to swallow. Did he really intend to rape her? Right here in front of everyone?

She wasn't going to get help from either of the women. Britta was too hysterical, and when Libby gaped at Kala, all she did was shrug. Not surprising, since she'd already made it clear she wanted nothing to do with the Klorthons.

Knowing there really wasn't anywhere for her to go didn't stop her from getting to her feet. When the warrior stepped over the hunter's unmoving body, she backed up until she bumped into a wall of large storage crates. With nowhere else to go and no one willing to stop him, she did the only thing she could. Prepared to give the asshole one hell of a fight.

#

Erak and his team hadn't stood a chance against the Klorthons who'd breached their ship. They'd been greatly outnumbered. Without control of his vessel, he'd been forced to surrender. Something about the timing of the attack bothered him. Why so soon after the commander's communication? It was almost as if the warriors knew they would be there, as if they'd been waiting for them. Worse yet was how they were able to get close enough to access the controls without setting off the ship's alert system. Once they were taken onboard the warriors' vessel, he'd been separated from Larn and Balok. The two males who'd tossed him on the floor had first taken him to see Molock. They'd spent hours beating him, and with great enjoyment when Erak refused to answer their leader's questions. Molock had seemed obsessed with finding the female Synge had taken from the Rivean colony. He'd also wanted to know how much hunter command knew about his operation, and if they'd sent reinforcements to find him.

Of course, Erak hadn't divulged any information. Each time he'd been beaten into unconsciousness, he woke to find himself on the floor in another storage area. He'd lost count after the third time he'd been questioned. Molock hadn't been present for the last beating. They hadn't asked any questions, so he assumed these two assholes had done it for fun.

Tarrons might possess accelerated healing abilities, but it didn't mean they couldn't feel their injuries. His head throbbed, and pain radiated through almost every muscle in his upper body. Besides his cut and swollen lip, he'd probably sustained damage to his ribs.

After overhearing the intended fate of Larn and Balok, he wanted to rip the Klorthons' throats out. Sending his friends to fight in the arenas was a guaranteed death sentence. Whoever was in charge of the fights was extremely intelligent and as elusive as the slavers. If the rumors the hunters had heard were true, the fights were being held on a ship instead of a planet. The constant movement of their location would explain why the hunters had never been able to find them.

Tamping down his anger, he forced himself to assess the current situation. He'd planned to remain motionless, hoping they would think he was unconscious and leave. He'd caught a brief glimpse of the human females before the warriors threw him on the floor. When he heard the warrior's intentions, he realized he had to do something to stop him. He opened his eyes and scanned his surroundings, glad his hair hid the movement.

He glimpsed the blonde human, the one named Libby, backing up against a large storage container, fear marring her lovely features. As a hunter, it was his duty to protect the women. A duty he would fulfill even if it cost him his life. As soon as the warrior stepped over him, Erak hooked the male's ankle and tugged.

The Klorthon lost his balance and fell forward. He snarled and rolled on his back, then struck out with his booted foot. Erak deflected some of the impact with his arm, but not enough to keep the male's boot from catching the side of his head, leaving him dazed.

The warrior got to his feet. "You will pay for that, hunter." His next kick hit Erak in his ribs, causing him to double on his side.

"Stop!" Libby screamed. She crouched on the ground in front of him, using her body to shield him from the warrior's attack.

What is she thinking? Why would she risk her life for his? She was too small. One blow from the Klorthon would surely kill her.

Using his remaining strength, Erak wrestled her around the waist and flipped her over him and onto her back. He covered her with his body, then braced for the warrior's assault.

"Enough. Molock will be returning from Tarron soon and wants him alive. I do not plan to lose my life because you cannot control your temper or your sexual urges. Now go."

Erak glanced over his shoulder to see the other male shoving his attacker toward the open doorway. Once the door closed, he released the female and rolled onto his back. With the new injuries, it was going to take a lot more time to heal. Until then, he wasn't going to be much use to anyone. A situation made worse without the aid of his team.

He didn't think they had a lot of time before the slavers arrived. Erak needed to find a way to notify command, and quickly. If they were not able to intercept his friends before they reached the arenas, then their fates were truly sealed.

Libby sat up and knelt next to him. "Hey, are you okay?" She pressed her palm against his cheek. The tenderness in her voice surprised him. It had been a long time since anyone had expressed an interest in his well-being. Even his own mother, too busy maintaining her political status, never took the time to bestow him with any acts of affection. When he was a child, she'd hired caregivers to look after his needs.

"I will survive." He stared at the alluring female hovering over him. Worry flashed in her amazing crystal-blue gaze. She was even lovelier than the image Ryos had sent him. Her golden hair hung loosely about her shoulders, tempting him to run his fingers through the silky strands.

"Why did you risk yourself like that? You could have been hurt," he said.

"Because you helped me, and I was afraid he would kill you." She worried her lower lip, the act so innocent yet sensual. It heated him to the core and made concentrating hard.

"I appreciate your concern, but do not ever do that again." Erak tried for a chastising tone but failed miserably. "You could have been badly injured, and it is my job to protect you."

"You're a hunter, aren't you?"

"Yes. How did you know?" he asked.

"Back on Rivean, before I was taken, another hunter helped

my friend when a Klorthon attacked her. He had similar markings."
She skimmed the skin on his shoulder with her fingertip.

The gentle touch made him shudder, spreading a wave of
warmth through him.

"Were you sent here to find us?"

"Yes, though I fear I have not been much help."

"You kept the warrior from attacking me. I'd say that was
very helpful, and I am very grateful."

Hope filled her expression. "Do you know what happened to
my friend Ricka? We were separated, and…"

"I am afraid I do not." He knew Synge had rescued a woman,
but he had no idea if it was the same female. The last thing he wanted
to do was give her false hope only to have her later learn something
bad had happened to her friend.

Overwhelmed by the need to comfort her, a feeling he hadn't
experienced in a very long time, he touched the side of her face. Her
skin was smooth and soft. He wondered if running his hands over
the rest of her petite form would be as enjoyable. "I will do
everything possible to find your friend once we are out of here."
Provided he was able to help them escape. Right now, the odds were
not in their favor.

He'd overheard the warriors talking during one of the
interrogation sessions when they'd thought he'd passed out. Those
responsible for capturing his ship had programmed the autopilot,
then sent the unmanned vessel in another direction. By the time
hunter command discovered there was a problem, the warriors'
vessel would have disappeared without a trace.

He rose up on his elbows, trying to push himself into a sitting
position. A burst of pain shot across his forehead, and his vision
blurred. He groaned and dropped on his back. The Klorthon must
have kicked him harder than he thought. There was no guarantee the
male who wanted Libby wouldn't return to finish what he started.
Erak needed to stay conscious if he planned to keep her safe.

#

Libby wasn't necessarily a coward, but she wasn't heroic
either. Throwing herself in front of someone to protect them was not
something she'd normally do. The hunter had stopped the warrior

from attacking her, and she hadn't been willing to stand by and see him be punished for it.

She also wasn't going to ignore the fact that he was injured more than he would admit. She hadn't missed the flicker of pain in his expression, or the loss of color to his exquisitely golden skin tone. "Why don't we get you off the floor. It has to be uncomfortable." She touched his shoulder, one of the few places he didn't have any bruises. "Can you stand without help?"

"No. Leave me here. I will be fine."

Stubborn male. Is he kidding? "Are you saying that because you can't move, or to be macho and difficult?"

"I am not familiar with this word 'macho.'"

Translation—pain in the ass. "Never mind, we'll assume you are in too much pain to move." She frowned, then glanced over her shoulder at Kala, who was standing several feet away. "Help me get him on a cot." When the woman ignored the request, Libby snapped, "Now."

Kala pursed her lips. "He said he would be fine."

"I don't care what he said. I'm not leaving him on the floor. Now get over here."

"You are very bossy, human." Kala walked over and knelt on his other side.

Libby had a sarcastic reply about stating the obvious on the tip of her tongue, but refrained from using it. "As I've already told you, the name is Libby. Please stop calling me human."

"As you wish."

They each grabbed one of his arms and braced his shoulders as they helped him to his feet. Once standing, he staggered a little but managed to make it to the nearest cot. His large frame completely covered the bed and his feet hung over the edge. The beds had obviously been designed to handle the smaller size of most women.

"Thank you." Libby glanced across the room. Britta was still sitting on her cot whimpering softly, her tiny frame tucked into a ball, her expression a blank stare. She was probably in shock and needed to be looked after. Of the two, the hunter was far worse and needed her immediate attention. "Why don't you check on her? She doesn't seem to be doing very well." She motioned her head toward Britta.

Kala made an exasperated noise, the first time Libby had seen any kind of reaction from the woman. "Humans are too emotional."

She took a seat next to Britta, then patted her back. "Everything is going to be all right." She shot Libby an inconvenienced are-you-happy-now look.

Satisfied, Libby turned back to the hunter. Snagging his discarded shirt from the floor, she folded it several times before placing it under his head. She examined his chest, hating what the Klorthons had done to his extremely handsome body. "They messed you up pretty badly. I'll be right back." She walked across the room and lifted the pad off an empty bed. Grabbing one of the corners, she made a hole in the fabric casing, then tore it along the side. After removing the covering from the thin mattress, she ripped it into smaller pieces.

She hadn't seen any med kits but remembered the partially empty water container she'd saved from her food tray and hid on the floor underneath her cot. The living conditions weren't great, but at least the warriors weren't starving them.

After grabbing the water and makeshift rags, she returned to the hunter's bed and knelt on the floor beside him. "I'd like to clean up your wounds, if you'll let me."

He stared at her curiously for a moment, then nodded.

"It's only water, but it will have to do." She opened the container, tipping it sideways to dampen one of the cloths.

"Please let me know if I'm hurting you, okay?" Starting with his forehead, she gently wiped the fresh and dried blood from his skin. She was well aware that he scrutinized her every move. His catlike eyes possessed the most amazing amber hue, and she couldn't resist meeting his gaze. "What should I call you?"

"Erak," he said.

"I'm Libby."

"Yes, I know."

"How did you…" She glanced at Kala, remembering the way she'd chastised her earlier. "Oh yeah." She paused for a moment. "Thank you again for helping me. I don't even want to think about what would have happened if you hadn't been here."

"Thanks are not necessary. As I stated before, I am here to protect you."

"Right."

Libby ran her fingertip along his lip, amazed at how quickly the cut was healing. "This looks quite a bit better."

23

Erak made a noise between a moan and a growl, then wrapped his hand around hers. The heat from his touch jolted her system, sending spirals of need straight to her core.

He quickly released her hand, and she wondered if he'd experienced the same reaction.

"Tarrons have accelerated healing. With some rest, the majority of my injuries will be barely noticeable within a few days," he said.

Libby picked up a fresh cloth and concentrated on cleaning his chest, trying to be as careful as possible. He didn't say a word, but she could tell by the way he winced that some of the wounds were deep and causing him a lot of pain.

After she finished, Libby picked up the water container and dirty pieces of fabric. "If you need anything else, let me know."

He closed his eyes without a response. Annoyed and a little hurt by his dismissal, she got to her feet. Libby wanted to check on Britta and see if there was anything she could do to help her. She'd taken only a few steps when Erak said, "I am indebted to your kindness. Thank you."

CHAPTER THREE

"Erak, wake up." He heard Libby's panicked voice and felt her hands shaking his shoulder. Shortly after she'd tended his wounds, he'd drifted in and out of sleep, waking several times to discover the female had remained close by, watching over him.

The ship's metal hull vibrated, along with the bed underneath him. He fought through the foggy haze in his mind and found her standing next to him.

"Something's wrong," Libby said.

An alarm blared through the confines of the bay, announcing a breach to the vessel's exterior.

"What's happening?" Britta shrieked, having recovered from her bout of shock. She shot up from a sleeping position and clutched her legs to her chest.

He pushed himself off the cot. Ignoring his rebelling sore muscles, he slipped on his shirt. The emergency power must have activated since the ship's gravity was still functioning. If the slavers had arrived, they would have been allowed to dock without triggering an alarm. This was something else, and probably not friendly. "I fear the ship may be under attack." Worried about the women's safety, he pointed at the gap between the large storage containers secured at the back of the bay. "I want you to hide between those crates. Do not come out until I tell you it is safe. Do you understand?"

"Yes," Libby nodded, grasping Britta's hand and helping her to her feet. They followed Kala, who was already doing as instructed.

Erak had no way of knowing the ship's location. If the

Klorthons had entered another quadrant, they could easily be traveling through an area monitored by space marauders. If they'd been boarded by outlaws, it wouldn't be long before they reached the cargo bays searching for anything valuable. The thieves weren't governed by morals. They'd take what they wanted, and kill for sport. The female's fates would be far worse than if they'd ended up with the slavers.

Erak glanced around and found nothing he could use as a weapon. He was good in a hand-to-hand fight, but not unarmed against someone with a laser weapon. He took a stance near the sealed door, surprise the only advantage he had.

He didn't have long to wait before the panel slid open. "I will retrieve the females and meet you in the launch bay. Get the shuttle ready to leave." He recognized the voice of the Klorthon who'd tried to attack Libby. He'd be damned if he'd let him get near her again.

Another warrior responded, "You need to hurry. It will not take the hunters long to reach this part of the ship."

Hunters? This was a rescue, not an assault. He remained hidden and alert, knowing the females were still in danger. The second the warrior stepped into the room, Erak launched the full weight of his body against him. Surprised, the male stumbled sideways, but not fast enough to keep from being slammed into the wall.

Recovering quickly, Erak doubled his fist and punched the warrior in the jaw. Erak wrenched the weapon out of his hand, then punched him again, the hard blow knocking him out.

He checked the outside access. Satisfied there were no other threats, he spoke to the females. "You can come out." He motioned for them to follow him. "We need to go."

As soon as they were all outside the room, he activated the door, locking the unconscious warrior inside. Erak took the lead and headed down the passageway. "Stay close behind me." He glanced over his shoulder. Libby had Britta's hand and was pulling her along as if she were a frightened child. Kala followed behind them, the straps of her shoes dangling from her hand.

They came upon a junction where a separate passageway veered to the right. A rhythmic pounding on metal alerted him to someone's approach. He held up his hand and signaled the women to stop, then aimed his weapon at the opening. A male, whom he easily recognized, cautiously moved through the opening. "Kel."

A grin spread across the other man's face. He lowered his repeater, then pulled Erak into a tight embrace. "My friend. You are not dead."

Erak couldn't be happier to see the man he'd known since childhood. "Thank you for stating the obvious."

Kel chuckled. "I see captivity has not improved your disposition any. You are still as cranky as ever."

"And you are late as always."

"We would have gotten to you sooner if the warriors hadn't used your ship as a decoy," Kel said.

"Then how did you find us?"

"The Klorthons hid this vessel behind one of our moons. They must have panicked when we captured their landing party, and decided to leave. It made it easy for us to track them."

"What about Molock? He was headed for Tarron," Erak said.

"Molock is dead. The man was stupid enough to go after a human female under Synge's protection."

Erak knew from experience that if someone was under his care, Synge would kill to protect them. He was sorry to have missed seeing the fight, especially after the beating he suffered from the Klorthon's orders.

Kel's gaze moved past Erak, and his smile widened. "Leave it to you to find a way to be locked up with a beautiful female."

Erak turned to find the women standing close behind him. Kel walked around him and held out his hand. "I am Kel, and you must be Libby?"

"Yes." She reluctantly gave him her hand.

"You are way more stunning than your picture. I would be honored to escort you to our ship."

A flush of pink brightened her pale cheeks. "Thank you, I…"

Friend or not, if Kel didn't release her hand, Erak was going to pummel him. Confused by his own reaction, Erak ran a hand through his hair and suppressed the urge to growl. "She is under my protection. I will see to her safety." He pushed his way between them. "I left a warrior in one of the storage bays. You might want to send someone to retrieve him."

Kel didn't bother to hide his amusement. "Of course."

Kala sidled up to Kel and hooked her arm through his. "Hey,

handsome. I would love an escort back to your ship."

He grinned. "It would be my pleasure."

"Does this mean we're going home now?" Britta, who'd been clinging to Libby's side, took a step closer to Kel.

"It does. Please follow me."

Outside the docking chamber leading to his ship, Kel pulled Erak to the side. "Ladies, please go inside. We will be with you shortly." Once the females had boarded and were out of earshot, his friend's expression sobered. "We did not find any sign of Larn or Balok. Where are they?"

"Molock sent them to the fighting arenas," Erak said.

"Fuck." Kel rubbed his temple. "How long ago?"

"I have no idea. I assume shortly after we were taken."

"Probably three days, then. I will contact command immediately and see if they can still track and intercept."

Erak followed him into the ship, weighed down by guilt and the knowledge that they were probably too late.

#

After they reached the hunter's ship, they were led to a smaller shuttle and told they'd be taken to the city of Madradie on the planet Tarron. Other than Kel and Erak, Libby had learned the remaining crew would stay behind and finish apprehending the Klorthons and secure their vessel.

The trip to the hunter command facility had taken less time than she'd expected. Once they landed, Erak appeared at her side, and led her off the shuttle to a transport. "So what happens now?" she asked.

"You will be escorted to the medical building, where someone will answer your questions and see to your needs."

"Are you coming with us?" The thought of never seeing him again bothered her more than it should.

"I am afraid not." He lifted his hand as if he were going to touch her, then dropped it to his side. "Do not worry. You will be provided with the best care and safely returned to your home."

"What about my friend Ricka?"

"I will make inquiries and send you word as soon as I have

any information."

"Thank you. I would appreciate it." Libby was a little disheartened that he wouldn't take the time to inform her personally. Why should he? He was doing her a favor and had his own life to get back to. She turned to follow Britta and Kala to a waiting transport.

During the short drive, Libby had stared at the landscape, amazed by the abundant collection of trees and foliage in the most stunning shades of yellow and turquoise. Unlike the Rivean landscape with its dry air, heavy rock terrain, and sparse plant life, a dense forest surrounded the perimeter of the facility.

She'd also noticed a difference in the air. It felt heavier, denser, and she'd been forced to take deeper breaths. During Libby's examination, the Tarron woman assigned to her explained the atmosphere was not lethal to humans, and her body would adjust in a day or two.

After she finished with the medical team, she'd been given clean clothes and shown to a bathing room to shower. Even though she had to roll up the sleeves on the shirt and the pant legs were too long, she was grateful to be wearing something clean.

A short while later, she'd been reunited with Britta and Kala. They were taken to a room that reminded her of a cafeteria, and provided with foil packets containing processed fruits and meats. Libby took a seat at a table near a large window so she could enjoy more of the landscape and observe the outside activities.

Britta plopped down in a seat opposite her and tore open her packet. "Can you believe all they have to feed us is this processed stuff?"

Kala sat at an adjoining table. "Stop whining, human. You should be thankful they did not leave you with the Klorthons." She flipped her hair over her shoulder. "I would have."

Britta gritted her teeth, then spoke to the hunter who'd been assigned as their escort. "How much longer before I can return home?" She shot Kala a disgusted glare. "And get away from her."

"Arrangements are being made for a temporary dwelling where you will stay until transportation back to Rivean has been secured," he said.

Kala didn't seem bothered by Britta's remark. She took a bite of the dehydrated meats. "Delicious."

Libby covered her mouth, trying not to laugh. It was hard not to like the Rhylarian, or appreciate her antics. The woman's unusual way of viewing the world was definitely growing on her.

"Libby." She recognized the deep voice of the man she thought she'd never see again. Her heart rate notched higher, and she shifted in her seat. Erak stood in the doorway, his expression pensive. His long hair was nicely groomed, and he wore a fresh uniform. She didn't think it was possible for the man to get better looking.

#

Surprisingly, Erak had wanted to escort Libby to the medical facility. Watching her get into the transport and knowing it was the last time he'd see her had caused an ache in his chest. He chastised himself for forming an attachment to the female. He had to accept the inevitable and push her from his thoughts. She would be returning to her life on Rivean. A life he wasn't a part of.

Kel had suggested—more like insisted—he go home and get some rest. Erak had lost too much time being trapped inside the Klorthon vessel. The last thing he wanted to do was return to the solitude of his dwelling. Instead, he'd showered and changed into a spare uniform. He headed to one of the terminals used for accessing information with the intention of checking the status on finding Larn and Balok.

Afterward, he planned to find Synge and question him about the female he'd rescued. He'd promised Libby he'd help find her friend. It was a promise he meant to keep, and one he could honor without being around her or the temptation she presented.

He'd barely had time to engage the system before his communication device beeped, alerting him to an incoming message. Glancing at the small screen, he frowned. Ryos had sent an order for him to retrieve Libby and bring her to his office.

Erak knew she'd already been assigned an escort, one who was quite capable of delivering her to the commander. Requesting an explanation would do him no good. He'd been given a directive and was expected to comply immediately. He had no idea why Ryos would want to see her, but he wasted no time in tracking her down.

He found her in one of the eating areas used by the medical personnel. She was sitting near a viewing pane, observing the other two females. She'd showered and changed. His breath hitched. Even though the clothes were too big for her petite frame, he still found her very appealing. He stared at her for several minutes before he finally spoke her name.

She turned in her seat, her lips curling into a cheerful smile. "Erak, what are you doing here?"

"Commander Davenger has requested to see you. I have been asked to be your escort."

"Oh, okay," she said warily.

Torin, the hunter currently assigned escort duty, shifted his stance. "What about the other two?" His normally rigid tone held a pleading quality. He obviously wasn't thrilled with having to spend time with the females.

"My orders only apply to the one." Erak could sympathize with the other man's plight after overhearing the females' argument.

"If you will come with me." He waited for Libby to get up, then led her out of the room and down a long hall.

"Do you know why the commander wants to see me?" Libby asked.

He struggled with the need to ease her worry, but refrained from taking her hand. "I was not informed, but you have nothing to fear. You are safe here." *I will not let anyone harm you. Ever.*

Two hunters, deep in conversation, approached them from the opposite direction. They both stopped and stared at Libby, not bothering to disguise their interest. Very few human females, especially ones as good-looking as Libby, visited the facility. She nervously crossed her arms over her chest and moved closer to him.

Unable to control the urge to protect her, Erak glared at the men and growled. They quickly looked away and hastened to move around them.

Libby gaped at him. "Did you just…"

He knew what she was going to ask, but offered no explanation, unsure why he'd reacted the way he did. "This way." He placed a protective hand against her lower back, enjoying the surge of warmth skittering across his skin. He activated the sensor to open the door, then led her into the commander's receiving area.

Darnay, the commander's assistant, sat behind a control display. She glanced at them and scowled. It was the same tight-lipped expression the older Tarron female had worn for years. Erak couldn't remember ever receiving a greeting from her, much less witness anything other than a frown. "Go inside. The commander will be with you momentarily," she ordered in her usual emotionless tone.

#

Libby hadn't appreciated the dirty look she'd gotten from the other woman. Before she could ask Erak what her problem was, he ushered her into another room. All thoughts of arguing with the older woman vanished the minute she saw the one person she feared she'd never see again. The best friend she considered family.

"Oh my God. Are you okay?" Ricka's strong arms encircled her in a hug. "They didn't hurt you, did they?"

Libby blinked back the threatening tears and clung to her friend. "I'm fine…" Her voice wheezed through the choke hold around her neck.

Ricka finally released her. "I didn't think I'd ever see you again."

"You can thank Erak." Libby turned and placed a hand on his arm. "He kept me safe until the other hunters arrived."

Ricka embraced him in a similar strangling hold. "Thank you so much for taking care of my friend."

Pink blossomed across Erak's sharply defined cheeks. He curled his hands into fists and shifted his feet. After a few moments, he patted her on the back. Libby didn't think anything could make the strong, brooding man more appealing until she saw his uncomfortable reaction to Ricka's display of affection.

"I think you have embarrassed him enough," said a male voice from behind her.

Libby had been so happy to see her friend, she hadn't noticed anyone else when they'd entered the room. She shifted sideways and found the man she'd served the night of her abduction. "You're that hunter from the bar on Rivean."

"Yes, and I am glad to see you have been returned safely."

Ricka slipped an arm around his waist and gazed up at him lovingly. "This is Synge. He's my mate…husband. He rescued me from that asshole Molock after you were taken."

"Congratulations, that's wonderful." Libby grinned, remembering the way the two had watched each other that night. She was glad to see it had turned out to be something more.

Even though she was extremely happy for her friend, she couldn't help feeling a little disappointed and lost. Before being abducted, they'd had a plan to return to Earth. Now that Ricka was mated, she couldn't expect her friend to go with her. The idea of going back to Rivean alone held no appeal. She had no clue what she was going to do now.

Before she could spend any more time worrying, the door slid open, and a large Tarron male walked into the room. He stood well over six feet and was several inches taller than the other two men. Libby caught a glimpse of something dangerous and predatory behind his carefully maintained smile. The dark red fabric of his uniform fit snugly against a broad chest. Golden hair draped across his shoulders. The four-inch scar running from his cheekbone to his jaw accented rather than marred his ruggedly handsome features.

"Commander." Erak stepped to the side, making room for him to enter.

He walked into the room, nodding at both men, then focusing his attention on her. "You must be Libby. I am Ryos Davenger."

"A pleasure to meet you."

"My apologies for being late, but I was detained by a communication from the colony." He held out his hand and gestured toward the large virtucom on the wall. "There is a representative waiting to speak with you."

Dread slithered along her spine. Why would anyone from the colony need to talk to her? She glanced at her friend.

Ricka shook her head. "I have no idea."

Libby nervously turned toward the screen. Ryos tapped several buttons on a nearby panel, and Boyd Keagan's image appeared in front of her.

Her stomach muscles formed a tight knot. *Why the heck does he need to speak with me?*

"Libby, honey. I was so worried about you."

"Why would you be worried about me? I hardly know you." And what was up with the endearing term?

"Can't a guy worry about his fiancée?"

The air whooshed from her lungs. "What are you talking about? I am *not* your fiancée."

"According to the bride contract you signed with the corporation, you are now. There's a clause in the fine print that states if you become a widow before the original marriage reaches the three-year mark, then someone else can petition to take you as a wife."

How she wanted to take a swipe at the smug smirk, the one she'd grown to hate. She rubbed her hands against her thighs, fighting for some composure. "You can't be serious." Her memories of the clause were vague, having dismissed the thought of anyone trying to enforce it.

"I'm very serious, darling. I submitted a petition, and it has been approved. We're going to be married."

Of course it had been approved. Why wouldn't it be? His uncle owned the damned mining company and would do anything for his brother's offspring. Hell, Dale Keagan had probably been the one to point out the clause in the first place. She didn't think for a minute Boyd was smart enough to find it by himself.

Libby cursed the day she'd run out of options. Times were hard and jobs were nonexistent in her hometown back on Earth. After eight years, she'd been laid off from her librarian position with no new prospects. Though they'd never been close, her married older sister offered her a place to stay.

The couple's situation wasn't much better. They had three kids and were barely making ends meet. As much as Libby appreciated the offer, she hadn't wanted to add to their already heavy financial burden. She'd had the crazy notion to sign up for the bride program, convincing herself it would be an adventure and fix all her problems. It had been an adventure, all right, just not the one she'd imagined.

"I have to complete a shift cycle, so it will take me about a week to come and collect you." He winked and swiped his tongue over his lip. "I can't wait to get you home and in my bed. See you soon." The link disconnected, and his image faded.

Oh God, this can't be happening. Struck with a woozy sensation, she struggled to remain standing. Luckily, Erak placed an arm around her waist and kept her from falling. "Are you all right?" He helped her sit in a nearby chair. "You do not look well."

Libby held his concerned gaze. "I…" Nothing else would come out. She couldn't find the words to tell him this was way worse than the threat of being sold to slavers.

#

The color drained from Libby's face, and Erak feared she'd slip into unconsciousness. She might not be his responsibility any longer, but it didn't mean he wasn't concerned about her welfare. It was obvious by her reaction she wanted nothing to do with the colony male. Listening to the other man rudely profess his intention to bed the lovely female sickened Erak. The thought of him, or any male, touching her had him clamping a tight rein on his anger. It was a good thing Boyd was on another planet. If he'd been in the room, he would be picking himself up off the floor.

Ricka scooted a chair next to Libby and took a seat. "Sweetie, are you going to be all right?"

Libby inhaled deeply, a bit of pink returning to her cheeks. "I think so."

Ricka gripped her hand. "I don't care if Boyd's uncle does run the colony, that asshole is not going to get away with this." She directed her attention to Ryos. "Isn't there anything you can do to stop him?"

"I am afraid not. She is neither a Tarron resident nor a claimed female. Because of the contract, she is legally a citizen of the colony, and as such, our laws prohibit interference in these matters."

"What is a claimed female? Does that mean married?" Libby asked.

"Not exactly," Ricka said.

"In our culture, a male can submit a claim for a female. A proclamation of their intent to eventually mate or join. If she accepts, the female is protected from being claimed by another male. Since this other male has stated a claim, there is nothing I can do," Ryos said.

"I see." Libby's disheartened tone troubled Erak.

"Can she at least stay with us until this is resolved?" Ricka asked the commander.

"I am sorry, but that will not be possible. She is a visitor, and it is my responsibility to ensure she remains in the city and is given appropriate care." Ryos moved away from the display panel and took a seat behind his desk. "She is human. Once her claim status is known, some males may become persistent in obtaining a joining. She will also need to be readily available in case one of the colony officials wishes to speak to her again. We cannot afford for them to believe we will prevent her return."

As a diplomat's son, Erak understood what Ryos wasn't saying. They couldn't do anything to jeopardize their strained relationship with the mining company or further irritate the human commander of the colony patrol. The male, on more than one occasion, had voiced his opinion about his hatred for all alien species.

"Which is why I am assigning her care to Erak," Ryos said.

That was the last thing he'd expected to hear. He'd assumed she'd be assigned to go with caregivers, an older couple more suited to see to her needs. Not an unmated male who lived alone. "What? Sir, no... Do you think that is wise?" He regretted the response as soon as he noticed Libby's hurt expression.

Ryos quirked his brow. "Are you questioning my decision?"

Yes. "No, sir." Rescuing her and protecting her during a life-threatening situation was one thing, but to be alone with her in his home—quite another. She was extremely beautiful, and he'd already fantasized about what it would be like to have her in his bed. *No, not a good decision at all.*

Libby got to her feet. "Wait a minute. Don't I have a say in the matter?"

"At the moment, I am afraid not. I believe you have been through enough, and the last thing I want is for you to be mistreated. Erak's parents are well-known emissaries for Tarron, and the colony would be less likely to offer a dispute if you were staying with him." Ryos rubbed his chin contemplatively. "You appear to be comfortable in his presence, but if you would prefer, I can assign your care to another officer. I will at least allow you the choice."

Erak could tell she was weighing her options by the way she glanced between him and the commander. He hated that his immediate reaction to the proposal hadn't been positive, and he wouldn't blame her if she chose to go with someone else. The thought of Libby being cared for by another hunter churned like acid in his gut. He could honestly admit he wouldn't be happy if she was staying with caregivers either.

The room remained silent, the tension mounting, everyone waiting for her answer. Finally, and with a little reluctance in her voice, she said, "I will go with Erak."

He blew out a relieved breath.

"Good, then it is settled," Ryos said.

Synge held out a hand to Ricka. "We need to leave. Arno and Teah are waiting for us."

"I am not going home and leaving my friend." Ricka got to her feet and poked him with her finger. "And don't you dare pull out those damned cuffs."

"I would not think of it. I assumed you would want to be close to her, so I made arrangements for us to stay in the city for a couple of days."

Ricka threw her arms around his neck and kissed his cheek. "I knew there was a reason I loved you." She released him and turned to Libby, pulling her into a hug. "Don't you worry. We'll figure out something to keep Boyd away from you. I promise."

"Thanks," Libby said.

Ricka turned to Erak. "I appreciate everything you've done, but if anything happens to her, you'll have to answer to me." She pinned him with an intimidating glare. "Let's just say I have a new knife and know how to use it."

Synge groaned, encircled her waist with his arms, and turned her around. "Do we need to have another discussion about who you can threaten with that damned blade? Do not make me sorry I replaced the old one." He tweaked her chin. "I have known Erak for a long time. I would trust him with my life and have no doubt he will take care of your friend."

Ricka directed her attention to Erak. The female's glare was frightening, making it clear she was waiting for some kind of reassurance. "You have my word. No harm will come to her."

Apparently satisfied, she let Synge pull her toward the door, giving Libby a quick glance over her shoulder. "I will contact you later so we can make plans to meet tomorrow."

"That sounds great." Libby solemnly watched them leave.

"You have an interesting friend. Does she really know how to use a knife?" Erak asked.

"Absolutely," Libby and Ryos answered at the same time.

CHAPTER FOUR

Libby watched the fading sunlight through the viewing pane of the transport. How could things in her life have gotten so bad? She tried to relax and push the upsetting thoughts about Boyd from her mind. Hard to do with the ever-growing tightness in her chest.

Then there was Erak. Handsome, strong, protective. He made her feel safe, something she needed badly.

"What is Rivean like? I have never been there." He'd been quiet for so long, she was startled by his question.

He glanced at her with those intense catlike eyes a vibrantly rich color of amber. She could stare at them for hours and not lose interest. "The air is very dry. Hot during the day and cold at night. Most of the terrain is made of rock and dirt with very little plant life. Nothing as amazing as your planet. All the different shades of yellow and turquoise are extraordinary."

"Do you look forward to returning?"

At the moment, no. "Not really. Before I was abducted, Ricka and I were planning to return to Earth. Now that she has a mate, I don't know..." With Ricka happily settled and her only future prospect a forced marriage, she felt more depressed and alone than she did after Trey's death. She could probably find a way to leave Tarron—an illegal one—and return to Earth. She'd be in breach of her contract. Being a fugitive and spending the rest of her life in hiding was not an option.

Boyd's uncle controlled the colony patrol. She held no illusions he wouldn't have her tracked down to keep his nephew happy. The thought of being around the vile man for the rest of her life created another assault of nausea. She desperately hoped Ricka would be able to come up with an alternative plan.

Erak drove the vehicle along a winding roadway into a secluded area away from the other dwellings, then parked beside a large two-story structure. "This is my home." The house had a lustrous exterior in various shades of black and gray. A lot of the other buildings they'd passed were constructed with the same rocklike design.

Now that they had arrived, panic settled in her chest. It was the same overwhelming feeling she'd experienced the day she arrived on Rivean and Trey had first taken her home with him. Alone with someone she didn't know and no idea what to expect. The only difference between then and now was that Trey had wanted her to be a part of his life. To Erak, she was nothing more than an assignment. An assignment he didn't really want. She could have chosen to go with someone else, but she hadn't. An uncertain decision she refused to analyze too closely.

Erak glanced at her tight grip on the seat, then shifted so he was facing her. "What is wrong?"

She stared at the house and gulped more air into her lungs. "I'm not sure this was a good idea. What if your family isn't happy about having a guest for over a week?"

He pried her fingers loose and clasped her hand. "Please look at me." The timbre of his lowered voice soothed her.

She forced her gaze back to him. Some of her tension eased at the way his normally stoic and serious expression had softened. "Other than Marna, my old caregiver who comes periodically to clean and make sure I have plenty of food, I live alone. My sister and parents live elsewhere."

"What about a girlfriend? I'm sure she's not going to appreciate having me stay in your home."

"Please explain the meaning of girlfriend."

Okay, this was getting awkward. He hadn't released her hand, and the heat from his skin was working its way through her entire body. "A special woman you care for, someone you…" What was the term Ryos used? "A claimed female."

"You mean an intended mate," he said.

"Yes, I guess that's it."

"No, there is no one." A brief hint of sadness flashed across his features, making her wonder if he'd had his heart broken or also lost someone he cared about. "Please believe me when I say you will be safe here. I will not let anyone harm you."

"Okay," Libby said.

"We should go inside." He released her hand and got out of the transport, then patiently stood by her open door, waiting for her to exit.

I can do this. How tough could it be? If she could survive scary Klorthon warriors, then a few days with the most gorgeous man she'd ever seen in her life shouldn't be a problem. Forget that he looked like he could more than fulfill every one of her sexual fantasies. No, this wasn't going to be hard at all.

#

After leading Libby to the entrance of his home, Erak placed his hand on the security sensor panel and the door slid open. Two steps inside and he heard a banging noise coming from somewhere near the rear of the dwelling. Normally, if the house had been breached, an annoying alarm would be blaring through the structure. "Stay here." He held out his arm to stop her, then slid the repeater from his holster.

"Is something wrong?"

"I am not sure." He headed in the direction of the sound, checking his surroundings for any sign of movement. When he reached the food storage and preparation area, he heard a familiar female voice cursing, and stopped. He growled and holstered his weapon as he walked into the room. "Nyssa, what are you doing here?"

His sister, four years younger than his thirty years, was the only member of his family who would be upset if something happened to him. She stood on the counter and glared down at him with golden eyes several shades lighter than his. Checking on his safety had nothing to do with her unexpected visit. He'd contacted her shortly after boarding the rescue ship to let her know he was still alive.

"Trying to fix this light. I think there is something wrong with the sensor." She made a snatching motion. "Would you mind handing me the adapter thingy?"

"There was nothing wrong with the sensor before I left. And that was not what I meant." Used to interpreting her illogical terms, he picked up the thin piece of metal off the counter and handed it to her. "Why are you here and not in your own home?"

"Our parents are traveling again and will be gone for several weeks. You know how I hate to stay in that huge monstrosity by myself."

"You are not by yourself." Erak picked up the eating utensils she'd dropped on the floor, then placed them in the cleansing unit. "You have Marna." The older female was a permanent resident in his parents' home. Having been their caregiver, she'd been mothering them both since they were young. When Erak moved out on his own, she'd refused to stop taking care of him, which was why she stopped by weekly to clean and ensure his food unit was stocked.

Nyssa secured the panel to the ceiling, then jumped down from the counter. A good six inches shorter than him, she took a step back and lifted her chin. "She is visiting her son for a few days, so I chose to stay here."

"Where is your transport? I did not see it when I arrived."

She shrugged, snagging a piece of meat from a nearby plate. "I parked it behind the house."

He leaned against the counter and crossed his arms. "What is his name?"

"Who? I do not know what you are talking about." She walked to the back of the room and swiped her hand in front of a sensor panel. She smiled when the overhead light brightened the room. "Told you."

"The name of whatever idiot you are trying to avoid." The male in question was probably another admirer who'd discovered his sister came from one of the wealthy and prominent families in the city. He probably had delusions of claiming her to improve his status.

Nyssa's long hair was several shades darker than his and possessed thin copper streaks. The pale golden hue of her skin made the marks along her neck and shoulder more noticeable, a quality a lot of males found appealing. Add in the fact that she consistently wore outfits that showed more skin than fabric, and he wouldn't be surprised to discover she had more than one male sniffing around for her attention.

"Fine. His name is Bokar, and he thinks I am his true mate. I did not want to hurt his feelings. I thought if I stayed here for a few days he would lose interest and find someone else."

"You know you cannot hide here forever. Eventually, you will have to tell him to leave you alone." Erak patted his holster. "Unless you would prefer I had a talk with him."

She frowned and shook her head. "No, big brother, I am quite capable of handling my relationships."

"Sure you are."

Nyssa leaned to the side and peered around his shoulder. "Why is there a human female in your home?"

Damn, he'd let himself be drawn into his sister's drama and had completely forgotten about Libby. He turned around to find her curiously watching them.

"Tell me you found her on your latest mission and have finally claimed a mate." She threw her arms around his neck and hugged him. "I am so happy for you."

Erak gripped her wrists and pulled her loose. "No, I would never…" he sputtered. "She's…"

"Exquisite and clearly thinks you are being a sheraaat."

"Language."

"A what?" Libby asked.

"I believe the correct human translation is asshole," Erak said.

"Good to know." From the mischievous twinkle in her eyes, he assumed Libby was covering her mouth to keep from showing her amusement.

"Do not mind the arrogance or his cranky attitude. I blame my parents." His sister waved her hand and walked past him. "Hello, I'm Nyssa, his brilliant and charming sister. And you are?" She took Libby's hand and pulled her farther into the room.

Erak rubbed the bridge of his nose. "This is Libby. She is under my protection and will be staying here until her escort arrives from Rivean."

"You are from the mining colony? Do you know Ricka?"

"She's my best friend," Libby said.

"Awesome. I have not met her yet, but your friend is the mate of the bodacious Synge."

Erak shook his head. "You have known the man for years. I

am sure he would not appreciate having you call him bodacious. Whatever that means."

His sister rolled her eyes. "It means handsome hunk. You are just jealous that no one says that about you."

Erak pinched his sister's arm, and she squealed. "You will have to excuse her. She is obsessed with anything related to humans and Earth. Ever since she accessed some old history virtuals, she has been unbearable."

"It's okay." Libby giggled. "She's right. He is fairly good-looking. Though I would have gone with ruggedly handsome."

"Please do not encourage her." He enjoyed the sound of her laughter. Even with all the trouble his sister caused, maybe having her here would be a good thing. At least for his new houseguest.

"Why are you dressed like you came from the medical facility?" Nyssa asked.

"Because I did…sort of."

"Did you not have anything else to wear? Where are the rest of your clothes?"

"Nyssa," Erak groaned. "Boundaries. She has been through a lot and does not need to be interrogated."

Libby held up her hand. "It's fine, and no, I don't have anything else to wear. The Klorthons didn't really let me pack before they abducted me."

"You were kidnapped?"

"Yes, and your brother helped me escape."

Understanding dawned on his sister's face, and she glared at him. "Why did you not tell me she was one of *those* females."

"Probably because it is none of your business."

"Of course, it is. She is under your protection, right? That means, as your sister and a fellow hunter, I am duty bound to take care of her as well."

"Going through the training program does not make you a hunter," Erak said.

Nyssa ignored him and spoke to Libby. "You poor thing. They probably fed you something from those compressed food packs. Are you hungry?"

"I wouldn't mind something to eat."

"I bet you would like something better to wear too." Nyssa glared at him. "You cannot expect her to wear this ridiculous outfit until she leaves. We will need to get her some better clothes, but that can wait until tomorrow." She draped a comforting arm across Libby's shoulder. "I have something you can borrow for now. Let me show you to your room. I will prepare you some food, then you can tell me all about the warriors and my heroic brother."

Erak decidedly changed his mind. Taking another beating from a Klorthon would be less painful than dealing with his sister. If he was smart, he'd call his parents, and beg them to return home from their trip sooner.

CHAPTER FIVE

Compared to the cot Libby had been forced to use during her time on the Klorthon vessel, the large bed in her temporary room was luxurious. She must have been exhausted because it was the best night of sleep she'd had in a very long time.

Choosing to take a quick shower before going downstairs, she made her way to the bathing stall. Unlike the chemical misting unit at the medical facility, this one supplied real water. Actual heated water. The unit in her home on Rivean barely maintained its warmth for more than a few minutes. A panel at the far end of the enclosure held a colorful assortment of cleansers. She pressed buttons, dispensing samples until she found one with a fruity scent reminding her of strawberries. She literally moaned with pleasure and couldn't resist spending a little extra time enjoying the warm and soothing cascade.

Feeling refreshed and only slightly guilty for pampering herself, she toweled off and put on the loose-fitting top and pants Nyssa had loaned her. The overly long pants sat loosely on her hips. She rolled up the bottoms to keep from tripping. The top of the shirt dipped low across her breasts, and the hem barely touched below her belly button. No amount of tugging helped pull the fabric over the parts of her midsection she felt uncomfortable exposing. If she didn't think it would hurt Nyssa's feelings, she'd put on the oversized shirt she'd worn the day before.

She didn't miss her makeup since she rarely wore it, but not having a comb to get through her naturally curly, long hair was another matter. She used her fingers to straighten out the tangles.

Satisfied she'd done the best she could, she left the room and headed for the lower level. Halfway down the stairs, she heard voices and followed them to the serving room.

When she reached the doorway, she heard Nyssa say, "Go to work or do whatever you have to do. I will take care of Libby." At least his sister was using her name and not referring to her as "the human female" like the medical staff had the day before.

"That is what has me worried." The sound of Erak's deep, rather sexy voice made Libby's heart flutter. She pictured him glaring at his sister, arms stubbornly crossed, with a frown on his handsome features.

"You do remember that I have passed some of my battle training. I am perfectly capable of taking care of myself." Nyssa's voice grew louder and more irritated.

Libby walked into the room, hoping to prevent another argument between the siblings. "Good morning."

"Awesome, you are up." Nyssa eyed her from top to bottom. "My clothes are still a little big, but they are much better than what you were wearing."

Libby found the other woman's constant use of human terms delightful and humorous. Not normally devious by nature, she entertained the thought of teaching Nyssa a few more phrases to irritate her brother.

Erak stood on the opposite side of the counter. "I think she would look nice in anything she wears."

His admiring gaze had heat skimming along Libby's throat and cheeks. Had she heard him correctly? Was he really paying her a compliment? She searched his expression for signs of sarcasm but only saw sincerity. Even Nyssa appeared dumbfounded by her brother's comment.

Quickly recovering, his sister took her hand and pulled her toward an empty chair near a table. "First, we are going to eat, then I have a full day planned." She coaxed Libby to take a seat.

Erak groaned and clasped his hand over his heart. "Please tell me you do not plan to cook for her. I do not want to explain to the commander how she was poisoned on her first day here."

Libby suppressed a grin. Who would have guessed the extremely intense man had a sense of humor? Nyssa, on the other hand, did not seem impressed by his remark and pinned him with a narrowed glare. "Of course not. I brought the food Marna prepared for me, and stored it in your cooling unit."

"And the rest of your great plan?" Erak said.

"We are going shopping. As I pointed out last night, you cannot expect her to wear the same outfit every day while she is here."

"I am afraid shopping will have to wait. Everything I own is still on Rivean. I have no way to pay for new clothes. Maybe you can help me find a job. I worked in a bar and was a very good waitress." She hadn't yet decided what her plans were for the future. If she was able to free herself from the contract with Boyd, she'd need to be able to take care of herself.

The thought of returning to a lonely, dismal existence back on Earth didn't hold any appeal. So far, she liked what she'd seen of the planet and entertained the thought of making Tarron her home. Especially now that Ricka was happily married and had a life here.

Erak's expression sobered. "Finding work will not be necessary. I will provide you with whatever you need." He addressed his sister. "Use my accounts with the merchants."

Having accounts implied a level of wealth. Not one for taking handouts, Libby shifted uncomfortably in her seat. "I can't let you do that. I don't want to inconvenience you any more than I already have." She sounded more sarcastic than she'd intended.

"It is not a request. I said I would take care of you, and I plan to do so. I can accompany you and make sure you are properly looked after."

"Totally, not necessary." Nyssa pulled some containers out of the cooling unit and set them on the counter. "You hate shopping. It will make you crankier than normal."

"I am not..."

Seriously, these two are worse than children. "I'm sure we will be fine. Besides, Ricka will be joining us." The night before, after Libby had settled in, she'd contacted her friend on the virtucom in her new room. They'd talked for what seemed like hours. She was excited about spending more time with her. "I'm sure she can call Synge if we need any help."

"You are my responsibility," he growled.

Great, now he was angry with her again. Later, when he wasn't around, she planned to ask his sister what she kept doing wrong. If she didn't figure out how to keep from upsetting him, it was going to be a long and stressful week.

Erak opened a drawer beneath the counter and withdrew a communication device. Crossing the room with heavy strides, he crouched beside her. "If you need anything, I expect you to use this." He must have noticed her flinch, because his gaze softened. "Please." His tone was less abrasive. He set the object in her hand, curling his large fingers around hers.

"Okay," she mumbled, unable to think clearly when he was this close and smelled so good. A woodsy scent, very unique, and extremely masculine.

He released her hand and got to his feet. "Stay out of trouble. I mean it." He glared at his sister one last time, then left the room.

After Libby heard the panel of the front door click into place, she turned to Nyssa. "I know the culture and rules are different here. I have no idea what's considered acceptable and what's not. Can you tell me what I did to upset your brother?"

"I will teach you whatever you need to know, and you did nothing wrong."

"Are you sure? Because he seemed awfully mad."

"Do not worry about him. Some Tarron males, particularly the hunters, are all about honor. Mentioning that you would prefer another male to protect you probably insulted his massive ego." Nyssa opened a container and set the contents on two plates. "He will get over it."

Remembering the way he'd reacted, Libby found it hard to believe. "I get the feeling he really doesn't want me here. He sure wasn't happy when Commander Davenger asked him to take care of me."

"Do not take it personally. He is very guarded with his emotions, only allowing those he trusts completely to get close to him."

Nyssa flashed her a contemplative grin. "I think he likes you more than he would like to admit. Otherwise, he never would have brought you into his home."

If that were the case, the man had an unusual way of showing it.

#

Nyssa drove her transport through the city of Madradie. Libby listened intently as she pointed out landmarks and shared interesting tidbits about Tarron history. "There is a fabulous outdoor bazaar on the other side of the city where visitors from other planets bring all sorts of items to sell." She pointed to the right.

"Is that where we're going?" Libby asked.

"Oh no. Even I will not venture there without a male escort. Too many… What is the human phrase?" Nyssa tapped her chin. "Shady characters."

Good to know they were going somewhere safe. Libby was certain she'd surpassed a normal person's quota for dealing with dangerous individuals. Remembering how close she'd come to being sold to slavers reminded her about the Boyd situation. A situation she'd been fighting hard to forget since she got up this morning.

Nyssa turned down a wide road leading to a large pad. The area was partially filled with various sizes and styles of transports. "Where did Ricka say she would meet us?" Nyssa asked after parking and exiting the vehicle.

"She said she'd wait for us near the main entrance."

"Sounds good. We will have to walk from here. Transports are not allowed in the center of the city. It is not far."

Libby didn't mind traveling on foot. It gave her a chance to enjoy the surrounding landscape. The unusual trees and foliage were breathtaking. They walked along a paved path through a dense forest area until they reached a huge building that reminded her of the one-level shopping malls on Earth.

She loved how everything appeared so natural, not like the synthetic metal-and-wood buildings on Rivean. They always seemed so sterile. Once they passed through a large archway constructed with intricately carved wood and stone, she realized it wasn't one building after all. There was no roof. Instead, numerous smaller structures were linked together, forming a continuous chain of shops.

"Libby." She heard Ricka yell, and turned to see her wave as she walked toward them.

She smiled and returned her hug. It was so good to be around her friend again, especially after all the time Libby spent thinking she might have lost her. "This is Nyssa, Erak's sister."

"It is great to meet you."

49

"And you as well," Ricka said.

Nyssa scanned the surrounding area. "I know you are claimed, but I cannot believe your mate would let you come here by yourself."

Ricka rolled her eyes. "Believe me, it wasn't an option. I came with Teah and Arno." She pointed at the older couple approaching from behind them.

"Libby, Nyssa, this is Synge's aunt and uncle."

"Ladies." Arno tipped his head.

"As discussed, we will be at the learning center, which is not far from here. You three will stay together, and you…" Teah directed her gaze at Ricka. "Will contact us as soon as you are done with lunch. I do not want my nephew to think he cannot trust us to look after you."

"I promise." Ricka pulled the older woman into a hug. "Thank you."

Teah nodded at Libby and Nyssa, then let Arno lead her toward the entrance.

"I take it getting on her bad side would not be a good idea."

"It's an act. Underneath, she is a softy, but don't ever tell her I told you that."

Libby chuckled. "Not a problem."

"Are you ready to have lunch?" Nyssa asked.

"Starved," Ricka said.

"Then follow me. I know a great place where we can sit outside while we eat." Nyssa led them inside a shop and over to a counter filled with an assortment of prepared dishes. "Choose whatever you like. Most of the food is made from either fruits or meats found locally."

Libby pointed at one of the containers. "Are you sure this is meat? Because it looks like worms."

Nyssa laughed. "It is a little spicy, but it is meat. I promise."

Willing to trust Nyssa's recommendations, and not insult her new friend, Libby placed a small portion on her plate.

After making their selections, they found a table located in the shade underneath an odd-looking tree with a smooth blue-green trunk. A patch of what looked like yellow grass grew around its base. She couldn't resist leaning over and running her fingers through the velvety blades.

"So tell me, what is it like being mated to the bodacious Synge?" Nyssa asked once they were seated and a server had delivered their meals and drinks.

"Bodacious?" Ricka nearly choked on her water. She cast Libby a questioning glance.

"She has a thing about old Earth terms." Libby popped a piece of fruit in her mouth, enjoying the extremely sweet taste. At least she assumed the bright orange berry was fruit.

Several Tarron males strolled by, stopping to watch them before continuing on their way. A few moments later, a couple more men sat at one of the nearby tables and proceeded to gawk at them. Libby experienced the same wave of discomfort she had with the hunters the day before. She leaned toward Nyssa, keeping her voice low so only the two women could hear her. "Why are those guys staring at us?"

Nyssa glanced over her shoulder. "Human women are very rare, and Tarron males have a voracious sexual appetite. Ignore them."

"Okay." A little hard to do when one of them kept staring at her as if she were a delectable piece of chocolate.

Ricka glowered at the men, then moved her chair so it blocked Libby from their view. God, how she'd missed her overprotective friend.

"I'm so sorry Ryos wouldn't let you stay with us." Ricka took another sip of her drink. "How is Erak treating you?"

"Fine. He's been very hospitable."

"You are talking about the same guy I met yesterday, right?"

"He's not so bad." Libby remembered the way he'd complimented her, and his determination to make sure she was well cared for.

"I'm sure he's not, once you get past the scowl and the irritating attitude," Ricka noted with sarcasm, then turned to Nyssa. "Sorry, I didn't mean to insult your brother."

"No worries. You are only speaking the truth. He has been moody and uptight since he was young. I think it was because our parents are what you would call diplomats. They hold a high rank in our society and travel a lot. Erak and I were often left with caregivers during our growing years."

"That must have been lonely for both of you," Libby said.

"We had each other, and Marna. She is wonderful and still takes care of us."

"Is that why he became a hunter? To get away from the political life?" Libby could relate to being alone and wanting to find a place in the world.

Nyssa nodded. "He does not talk about it much, but I think he resents some of his assignments. Because of his family ties, the commander has him escort a lot of the visiting emissaries."

That would explain why he'd been so upset about being assigned to take care of her. He'd probably viewed her as another babysitting job. Yet for a brief amount of time this morning, he'd actually been quite charming. Even when he acted surly, being near the extremely handsome man warmed her from the inside out. Something she'd been working hard not to think about.

Despite his serious and controlled personality, the more she learned about Erak, the more she liked him. Crap, she had to be careful. The last thing she needed was to fall for the guy. "So, other than me becoming a fugitive, were you able to come up with anything to get me out of this mess with Boyd?"

"I spent most of the night reviewing the corporation's bride contract. According to one of the clauses, Boyd can't force you to be his wife if you are already in a binding commitment with someone else," Ricka said.

"I think I may have a way to help." Nyssa's excitement was infectious.

Unlike her brother, the younger woman was very easy to talk to. While Nyssa helped her get settled into her room the night before, Libby had told her about the problem with Boyd. "Really? How?" She tried not to sound too enthusiastic.

"We need to find a Tarron male who is willing to submit a claim for you. It would ensure your protection, and the colony cannot force you to return to Rivean."

"Meaning you can stay here and the asshole can't force you to marry him. That sounds like a great plan." Ricka placed a comforting hand on her arm. "I know you had your heart set on going back to Earth, especially after what happened to Trey. This can't be an easy decision, but I don't want you to leave. You're part of my family."

"I don't want to leave you either, at least not right away." It always amazed her how well Ricka understood her, even without having to say a word.

"Would I have to…you know, have sex with whoever you find?" Libby asked, knowing it would be a deal breaker for her.

"Not unless you want to," Nyssa said.

"But if I accept a claim, won't I be stuck with someone else I don't want?" Libby asked.

Nyssa slid her empty plate to the middle of the table. "No, the claiming is temporary. If after a certain amount of time you decide not to join, you can break the claim."

"How long will that be?" Libby asked, unsettled by the thought of being sent to live with another stranger.

"To be safe, thirty to sixty moon cycles at the most."

"Which is how long exactly?

"Translation, approximately two to four months," Ricka said.

"That's a long time," Libby slumped back in her chair.

"You really don't have much of a choice. Not unless you want to spend the rest of your life being mauled by Boyd."

"Thanks for the disgusting visual." *And the nauseous stomach.* "I guess I'm in. What do I need to do?" Libby asked.

"Nothing." Nyssa rubbed her hands together. "Leave the planning to me."

CHAPTER SIX

Erak tapped his fingertips on the control display, frustrated that Command still hadn't received any word from the team searching for Larn and Balok. Too much time had lapsed since they'd been taken, and tracking them was getting more difficult. Finding his friends might be impossible, but he was determined to keep searching.

Never a pleasant part of his job, he'd spent most of the morning compiling a report accounting for his time spent aboard the Klorthon vessel. The documentation should have been completed by now. Constant thoughts of Libby kept distracting him from the task.

Seeing her in the vivid green outfit this morning had almost been his undoing. He'd gotten hard staring at the creamy skin on the exposed portion of her belly and imagined what it would be like to run his fingertips across the firm surface. To make it worse, he'd gotten close enough to scent the hint of the cleanser she'd obviously used to shower with. On her, it was sweet and enticing. He couldn't remember the aroma ever smelling so good.

He knew some of the clothes worn by the females on his planet contained far less fabric than the outfit his sister had loaned Libby. The thought of other males seeing her in that outfit stirred his jealous nature. If not for his sister's presence and the argument it would have caused, he'd have prevented the alluring female from stepping outside his home.

Erak slipped the communicator from his belt. He rolled it in his palm, tempted to contact Libby and ensure the anxiety building in his gut was unfounded. An action he'd repeated at least ten times since arriving at hunter headquarters.

Spending some time alone with his sister would be good for her. His sister's friendly and outgoing personality, the complete opposite of his, had a way of putting people at ease. Something he was certain the troubled female desperately needed right now. He would give anything to have the same ability. The ability to make her smile, not see the despair she attempted to hide when he was around.

He didn't trust the colony officials and had asked the commander to access a copy of Libby's contract. Ryos had also supplied him with information on her marriage. Had she cared about the man she'd been married to for such a short time? He'd known she was a widow. Keagan, the rude sheraaat, had made sure to remind her during the transmission. Thinking about what waited for her when she returned to Rivean had him clenching his fists.

Boyd had been telling the truth, but he'd failed to mention an additional clause that would relinquish his rights if she were legally committed to another. Basically, if someone else provided some type of claim—an engagement or marriage—he would have no rights to her. Erak would claim her himself if he thought she'd accept his offer. Even though their time together had been short, he liked her and had formed an attachment to her. He was afraid he wouldn't be able to let her go after the temporary period ended. He couldn't deal with another rejection, not when the old wound Sharra caused still sliced like a fresh cut. He'd made a vow never to mate and he planned to keep it.

Synge appeared in the doorway, then leaned against the frame. "You look as if you would like to kill something, or someone. Anything I can do to help?"

"Not at the moment. No."

"I am curious. Why are you here? I thought you would be with my mate's friend," Synge said.

"She is shopping with Nyssa."

"You left *your female* alone with your sister?"

When did Libby become my female? Erak liked the sound of that more than he should. It triggered the protective urge he'd been experiencing since he'd met her.

"This is the same woman who goes around telling males they are bodaciously handsome, and is always concocting schemes. I agree with her good taste, but what were you thinking leaving my mate's friend in her care?"

Erak rubbed the back of his neck. "I thought Ricka was with them."

"She has already returned to our room. I am leaving now to spend the rest of the day with her. Which means…your sister could be anywhere, doing who knows what—around unmated males."

Fuck. He should have paid attention to his instincts. Erak jumped up so fast, the chair toppled over. "I really despise you right now." Hurrying from the room, he ignored the grating laughter echoing through the hall.

#

Libby was certain she was going to hyperventilate. She still couldn't believe she'd agreed to Nyssa's proposal to find someone to submit a claim. After lunch, the women devised their strategy, more like she listened and the other two worked out the details. The remainder of her visit with Ricka was spent catching up on everything that had happened since the night she'd been abducted. With a little reluctance and a lot of hugging, Ricka left when Teah and Arno came to escort her back to the suite of rooms Synge had acquired for them.

Afterward, she let Nyssa drag her into numerous shops searching for what Erak's sister called "the perfect outfits" and necessities. Libby's attempt to end the outing after they'd purchased a couple of days' worth of clothes failed. Nyssa made sure she had a wardrobe large enough to last her longer than a week. Libby planned to repay Erak for his generosity and kept a mental tally of all the rivets charged to his accounts.

"Shouldn't we be getting back? I don't want to give your brother another reason to be upset," Libby said.

"One more place, I promise. You will need a special gown to wear when you meet with potential suitors." Nyssa took her hand and tugged her toward a quaint little building hidden at the far end of the courtyard. "Do not worry. This will not take long at all."

Somehow she didn't quite believe the part about not taking much time, especially when Nyssa started haggling with the shopkeeper. Libby had finally reached the point of saturation. She lacked the energy to try on anything else and desperately needed to get off her aching feet. Remembering the bench they'd passed on their way to the shop, she headed outside.

She hadn't been seated long before a tall Tarron male stopped in front of her. Another man, big and intimidating, came up behind her and propped his elbows on the back of the bench inches from her left shoulder.

"Hello, pretty thing. What is a human female doing in this part of the city?" The one hovering over her crouched beside her, preventing her from leaving the bench.

She scooted sideways so she could see both men at the same time. They were dressed in similar dark pants, and sleeveless shirts stretched across thick-muscled chests.

The man behind her leaned closer and sniffed. "Attractive and unmated." He smirked and glanced at the other man. "She does not wear another male's scent. I think she is all alone."

"I'm not alone. I'm waiting for my friend." Libby tried to calm her racing heart, frantically praying Nyssa would get her ass out here.

#

Erak hadn't required any goading from Synge to imagine all kinds of scenarios involving Libby and other males. Did she really belong to him? The animalistic side of his nature continually surfaced, trying to convince him it was true. No matter how much he refused to believe it, he couldn't ignore the need driving him to find and protect her. He hadn't been able to reach either female via their communication devices or the virtucom in the transport, and his panic was steadily climbing.

Thankfully, the device he'd given Libby contained a tracker. It hadn't taken him long to locate the signal or follow it to the far end of the large market area. He entered the courtyard at the same time one of two males seized her wrist and jerked her off a bench.

"Let me go. I told you I am not alone," Libby yelled and struggled to break free.

All logic fled from him the minute he heard her pleas. Instead of following protocol and retrieving his repeater to warn the males away, he yanked the man accosting Libby backward, then slammed his fist into his jaw.

The man's head snapped to the right, and he dropped to the ground.

Erak pulled Libby behind him. "The female is under my protection. She belongs to me."

The man rolled on his side, clutching the side of his head. "What the... Hunter." His gaze locked on Erak, and he froze, fear dashing across his features. "I am sorry. I did not know."

Before the downed male could get to his feet, his friend was at his side, sporting an equally terrified expression. "Come on. We should go." He half dragged, half pulled the injured man to his feet. Without another word or a backward glance, both men took off running.

Erak turned around to find Libby shocked and staring at him. "Are you all right?" He ran his hands along her arms, needing the contact to calm him, to soothe him.

"I'm fine, but I wouldn't be if you hadn't..."

Nyssa came running out of the shop. "What happened?" She dropped her containers and rushed to Libby's side.

"Where were you?" Erak growled, enraged by his sister's negligence.

Nyssa glanced at the building behind her. "I was inside..."

"I do not care. You were supposed to take her shopping, then bring her home. Not keep her out all day." He rubbed the back of his neck, the action failing to relieve his tension. "You were not to let her out of your sight. Have you forgotten her status? Other males will be able to scent that she is unclaimed. She could have been taken, and forced to..."

Libby stepped between them, facing Erak. "Please stop. It's not Nyssa's fault. I left the shop without telling her where I was going. I didn't know about the...the scent thing." She placed her hand on his chest. "I'm sorry. If you want to be angry, be angry at me."

Being around Libby brought out emotions. Emotions he'd suppressed a long time ago and wasn't comfortable dealing with. He'd used his discomfort as an excuse to let Nyssa convince him he wasn't needed. His anger was misplaced, and he knew it. Libby was right; this was not his sister's fault. It was his. None of this would have happened if he'd gone with them today. He'd taken a vow to protect Libby, and he'd failed. Badly.

He wanted to shout his frustration. To tell her how the thought of any harm coming to her was making him crazy, but he couldn't. All he could do was stare, his throat constricted and incapable of forming words.

"I'd like to go back to your home now." She glanced at Nyssa, her expression stricken with unspoken sadness and apologies. After returning to the bench to collect her belongings, she walked past him and headed toward the main entrance.

Nyssa shook her head and hissed, "Sheraaat." Before he could respond, she picked up the items she'd dropped on the ground, then took off after Libby.

Erak pinched the bridge of his nose. Clearly, his sister was correct. He was an asshole.

#

Once they arrived at his home, Libby said she was tired and disappeared into her room. Shortly afterward, Nyssa announced she would be staying elsewhere for the night. Her way of letting Erak know she was still angry and didn't want to be around him. When it came to heated disagreements, his sister's temper equaled his own. He knew it would be useless trying to apologize until they'd both had some time to calm down.

Using work as a way to avoid dealing with his guilt, he spent several unproductive hours reviewing data on potential locations for the fighting arenas. He hadn't found anything useful to help him locate Larn and Balok, and no promising news had arrived from the search team.

Adding to his frustration was the memory of Libby's disheartened and pained expression. A pain he was entirely responsible for causing. Determined to apologize for his irrational behavior, he'd gone to her room. The door stood open, and the containers from her shopping excursion had been left on the bed, untouched.

A heavy weight settled in his chest. Had she been so upset, she'd decided to leave? He frantically searched every room. He reached the gathering room and caught a faint whiff of her unique scent near the door leading to the outside area behind the dwelling. He spotted her standing barefoot on the smooth rock surface leading away from the house. She'd wrapped her arms across her middle and stared at the evening sky, the twin moons bathing her in a golden glow.

He slowly approached her, clearing his throat so he wouldn't startle her. She glanced over her shoulder, acknowledging his presence, then returned to gazing at the sky. This was going to be more difficult than he'd hoped, but no less than he deserved. He paused to find the right words. "I would like to apologize for the way I behaved earlier."

"It's not me you should be apologizing to, it's your sister. She didn't do anything wrong."

As he'd expected, Nyssa had gained another friend. Libby's defense of his sister was admirable. "I know. And I will speak with her tomorrow when she returns."

"How do you know she'll come back?" She jutted her chin defiantly and slapped her hands to her hips. "What if she never wants to speak to you again?"

Erak wouldn't blame his sister if that was the case, though he knew better. They'd had many arguments over the years, some worse than this, and they'd always found a way to settle their differences. "Then I will...what is the word humans use for begging on their hands and knees?"

"Grovel."

"Yes, I will grovel."

"I can't imagine you as the groveling type." Her stance relaxed a little, and her hands slid to her sides.

"You might be right," he sighed.

She seemed to ponder what to say next by biting her lower lip. The sensual action caused him to harden painfully against the front of his pants.

"I think maybe I should be the one to apologize. The last thing I wanted was to make your life difficult or cause problems between you and your family." Moisture glistened in her eyes. "I will contact the commander in the morning and have him find somewhere else for me to stay." She ducked around him.

He caught her wrist before she could reach the doorway. "Wait, please."

When she stopped, he placed a hand on her waist and pulled her toward him.

"I...I do not want you to go."

"If that is true, then why are you always so angry whenever I'm around?"

"Because you make me feel things I do not want to feel."

"What kind of things?" Libby asked.

Every need, every emotion he'd experienced earlier surfaced again. Before he could stop himself, he'd slipped his hand into the hair at her nape and closed his mouth possessively over hers.

He expected her to resist. Instead, she relaxed in his arms and melted into him. He kissed her harder, tasting, taunting, teasing. Needing more, he parted her lips, delving his tongue deeper. Tightening the grasp on her waist, he ground his throbbing erection against her. She responded by moaning and slipping her arms around his neck.

He was so lost in the moment, he ignored the beep from the communicator attached to his belt. When the irritating noise persisted, he pulled away from her and unhooked the device. "This better be important," he snarled, turning his back on Libby.

"Am I interrupting something?" Kel asked humorously.

Fuck, he hated his friend right now. "What do you want?"

"I will take that as a yes." Kel laughed. "You told me to contact you as soon as I heard anything about Larn and Balok."

Erak's anger subsided. "Did the team find them?"

"No, but they may have found someone who knows the location of the arena. Hopefully, they will gain some useful information."

Over the past several years, the hunters had come across informants who were convinced they knew the arena location. So far none of them had been helpful. Maybe their luck had finally changed. "Let me know when you hear something," Erak said.

"I will." Kel disconnected the transmission.

He returned the device to his belt. "I am sorry..." His explanation fell on silent space. Libby was nowhere in sight.

CHAPTER SEVEN

"She is my responsibility, and she stays with me. Yelling is not going to make me change my mind." Erak glowered at his sister, then leaned against the edge of his desk at command headquarters. He'd already apologized to her for overreacting the day before—numerous times. He'd also informed her that under no circumstances was Libby going to be allowed to go anywhere without him. Luckily, Libby had excused herself from the room to give them time to talk and couldn't hear their heated exchange.

"I think you are being unreasonable," Nyssa said.

"I do not care."

Erak glared at his sister. "Since Synge is spending some time with his mate, I agreed to assist Dathan with the recruit training. You will not leave this building, and you will not get into any trouble." He pushed away from the desk. "Or do I need to assign you an escort as well?"

"You wouldn't dare."

He curled his hand around his communicator.

"Fine. We will not leave the building," she groaned, then stormed toward the door.

His sister might have agreed with him, but he knew better than to believe she would comply with his request. He'd already arranged for Torin to keep an eye on the women without alerting them to his presence.

The training session had taken less time than Erak had

expected. After finishing his shower and putting on a clean uniform, he looked forward to finding Libby and heading home early. He was halfway down the hall leading to his office when his communicator beeped.

Seeing Torin's name on the screen, he tensed. "Please tell me my sister did not try to leave."

"She is still here, but you might want to get your ass over to training area three." The link disconnected before he could ask what kind of problems she could possibly have caused now. With dread gnawing at his insides, he quickly changed direction. Reaching his destination in record time, he rushed into the room and nearly collided with a small group of hunters.

He pushed his way through to see what had attracted their attention. Dumbfounded and on the verge of losing his temper, he stared at Libby facing off with his sister on one of the training pads. Determination strained her features as she prepared to defend herself.

She'd secured her golden locks at the back of her head. Both females had changed their clothes, and his sister was wearing one of the outfits she'd been given when she'd enrolled for training. He wasn't sure what Libby was wearing. Whatever it was didn't have nearly enough fabric. Her arms, legs, and midsection were bare, exposing her shapely body. It explained why the group of males hovered inside the room.

She had no idea how exquisite she was, or how appealing. He wanted to drag her from the room. The last thing he needed was to cause a scene in front of his peers. It took every ounce of self-control to keep his pace slow and restrained as he walked across the room. "What do you think you are doing?"

Nyssa rolled her eyes and shook her head. "I thought it was obvious. We are training."

"I can see that, but why are you training with her and not an instructor?"

"There were none available. Besides, you told me we could not leave the building. After yesterday, we thought it might be a good idea if she learned some moves to protect herself." Nyssa swept some loose strands behind her ear.

He wanted to argue, to protest, but knew by the way they both glared at him it would do no good. Sweeping his hand in front of Libby, he asked, "Where did you find these clothes? They are not proper training attire."

Nyssa hooked a thumb over her shoulder, pointing at another human. The female sat on the floor, leaning against the wall and drinking from a water container. "Lyna loaned her the clothes. Apparently, it is what they wear on Earth when they are exercising."

Great. It was one of the recruits, the same woman Dathan had been arguing with earlier. "What does that mean?"

"Err...you are hopeless. It means training to stay fit. You should work on learning more Earth terms if you expect to interact with humans." Nyssa gave him a disappointed nudge. "Especially now that you have one living with you."

"I can communicate fine, and you are diverting the discussion."

"I believe you mean changing the subject." Libby attempted to hide her amusement.

She moistened her lips with her tongue. It reminded him how soft and pliable they'd been the night before, and a wave of heat burst through him. He shifted his attention back to his sister, pushing away his desirous thoughts before his groin had time to stiffen. "In any case, her attire is drawing attention."

"You are the one who brought her here." Nyssa leaned to her left to glimpse at the crowd of males. "I do not see how this is a problem. She does not want to go back to Rivean. If someone claims her, then she can stay." She wiggled her eyebrows. "And this is definitely a great place to find potential males."

Family or not, I am going to strangle her. Erak heard murmurs among the men. He didn't need to turn around to know what they were discussing. His sister had spoken loud enough for them to hear Libby wasn't claimed or mated. They probably already knew she was under his protection, and wouldn't attempt to remove her from the facility. Not unless they wanted to risk disobeying the commander's orders.

They could, however, approach Libby and present her with a claiming offer. An offer he couldn't prevent her from accepting.

He glared at his sister. "Please tell me you have not devised one of your schemes to help her."

Nyssa didn't answer, only shrugged and grinned.

"Unbelievable," he muttered, then turned his attention to

Libby. "You did not agree to this absurd plan, did you?"

"What if I did?" Libby asked.

Erak swept his hand through his hair, ready to pull it out. "You would seriously consider letting someone you do not know submit a claim for you?"

"It's not like I have a lot of options." Her forlorn expression tore at his heart.

He raised his hand to caress her cheek, then stopped when Commander Davenger's voice echoed through the room. "I believe you all have work to do."

Erak glanced toward the entrance in time to see the group of males flee from the room. Lyna also got to her feet and slipped through the doorway leading to a changing area.

As soon as the last male disappeared, Ryos approached them. "Greetings, Libby. It appears you are doing well."

"Yes, thank you."

Ryos raised a questioning brow. "Working out or training?"

Erak frowned, surprised that his boss understood the difference.

"Training. After what happened with the Klorthons, I wanted to learn how to defend myself. Nyssa was kind enough to teach me a few moves."

Erak was surprised and relieved she hadn't mentioned her unfortunate encounter with the two males the day before. He'd already beaten himself up with guilt. He didn't require a lecture from Ryos.

"I think it is a very good idea. It would be better if you had an expert assist you with the lesson. If you would like to continue, I will assign someone more qualified to work with you."

"I would like that, thank you."

There was no way Erak could stand by and watch another male teach Libby, knowing his hands would be touching her body. He started to argue, but Ryos clapped his shoulder, interrupting him. "I assume you will teach her the basics and ensure her lesson goes well."

What had just happened? "Yes, sir."

Ryos smiled at Nyssa. "If you have some time, Dathan is waiting in my office to review your training program."

"Awesome." Nyssa beamed with excitement.

"Good, then we will leave these two to train." Ryos headed toward the exit with Nyssa following close behind him.

#

Libby was tired of being a victim and had been thankful for the workout with Nyssa. She hadn't expected Ryos to agree to her training, and she certainly hadn't anticipated Erak being assigned the task.

He walked over to the entrance and activated the sensor to close the door.

"What are you doing?"

"Preventing any interruptions." He stalked toward her, each step predatory and a little unnerving. She now knew how a deer felt when hunted by a mountain lion.

Reaching the edge of the pad, he unhooked his weapon belt and set it on the floor. He slid off his boots, then removed his shirt. Libby couldn't stop staring at his bare chest, or those superbly ripped muscles. Muscles she desperately wanted to run her hands over since the first day she'd seen them. Other than a few scars, he'd completely healed from all the cuts he'd received at the hands of the Klorthons. "Don't you want to change?" She forced her gaze to meet his.

"I am comfortable." He stepped next to her on the pad. "Are you ready to begin?"

Hell no. She'd had a hard enough time paying attention to Nyssa because her thoughts constantly strayed to the intoxicating kiss she'd shared with Erak. How was she supposed to concentrate when he was standing this close and smelling so good?

All she could think about was how right and wonderful she'd felt tucked safely in his arms the night before. It didn't help that he looked as if he'd stepped off the cover of one of the romance novels she had stashed away in her living unit back on Rivean.

She took a position facing him. "What do you want me to do?"

"First, I am going to show you some simple techniques to free yourself if someone grabs your wrist. Then I will teach you how to escape a full-body hold."

"Sounds good."

As promised, he showed her several moves, patiently

explaining, then demonstrating the execution. After what seemed like hours, Libby stopped to rub her sore wrists.

"Are you in pain? I do not wish to hurt you."

"It's not bad," Libby said.

"Let me see." Erak took her hand, gently massaging it with his thumbs. He slowly worked his way along her wrist and forearm. "How does that feel?" He stopped manipulating her muscles but didn't let go of her hand.

Fantastic, wonderful, and please don't stop. "Much better, thank you."

"We can end the session if you are tired."

"I'd like to keep going."

He nodded. "I will show you one more move, then we will end for today."

"All right."

"Stand facing away from me."

Libby did as he instructed, then glanced over her shoulder. "How long have you been doing this? Being a hunter I mean?"

"A long time." He pressed his chest into her back, rubbing against her exposed skin, sending shivers along her spine. "The equivalent of eight Earth years."

"Isn't it kind of lonely? Don't you ever wish for more?"

He placed his arm around the front of her chest. "I do not have time to think about it. My job keeps me busy." A total lie. He'd thought about nothing else since he'd been assigned her care.

Using the move Nyssa taught her, Libby elbowed him in the ribs, causing him to loosen his grip. She spun around and grabbed his forearm, then braced her legs, using the momentum to flip him over her upper body. He dropped to the mat, groaning as he landed on his back. Moving quickly, she straddled his chest and pinned his arms with her legs. "You didn't answer my question."

Wrenching his arms free, he grabbed her waist and bucked his midsection at the same time. *Crap.* She lost her grip, and he easily rolled her onto her back and covered her with his body. His hips ended up between her spread legs, and he'd braced his arms on either side of her, preventing her from moving. Heat pounded through her, and she almost wished they were naked. "And you did not tell me my sister had already shown you this move."

He lowered his head until his face was inches from hers, then

67

brushed his lips across hers with the gentlest of kisses. Nuzzling the side of her face, he sniffed the length of her throat. "Are you...smelling me?" Libby asked.

"Yes."

"Why?"

"Your arousal is very enticing." Erak pressed a soft kiss to the base of her neck.

She tried to push against his chest. "I'm not...aroused."

He pinned her with one of his intense gazes, then moved his hips until his erection grazed the sensitive spot between her legs. Heat surged to her core, and before she could stop it, a moan escaped her lips.

"Really?" he asked.

Libby heard the door panel slide open and tilted her head back to see Nyssa and Lyna walk into the room. *Great.* She'd been caught making out by his sister. Could things possibly get any more humiliating?

"Did you know there was a problem with the lock? I had to override the sensor," Nyssa said.

Of course she did. Libby couldn't see what Nyssa had tucked into her pocket, but had a good idea it was what she used to open the door. "Sorry, didn't mean to interrupt." Nyssa grinned and tugged Lyna toward the mat. "How is the lesson going?"

Erak's body stiffened against Libby and a rumble erupted from low in his chest. He rolled to the side and got to his feet, pulling her with him. "We were finished. What do you want?"

"We are going out for drinks with some of the recruits and thought Libby should go with us. We might be able to find a male for her."

"No, she will not be going with you."

"You do know I can answer for myself."

"I do, but the answer is still no. You are under my protection. I would prefer not to fight a room full of males who may get overzealous in their pursuits to offer a claim for you." He aimed her toward the changing room. "Please go shower and change so I can take you home."

Libby remembered how he'd reacted when the two men had tried to abduct her. She was certain he'd fight to the death to protect her. She wasn't happy about him making decisions for her, but she didn't want to be responsible for him being injured either.

"Fine, you win." *This time.* She threw her hands in the air.

Libby dropped the towel she'd used to dry her hair. "So soon?" She swallowed back the anxious knot forming in her throat.

"We are running out of time. It was not easy finding a male I trust who will take on the task of claiming you." Nyssa leaned against the wall, her arms crossed, reminding Libby so much of Erak. His sister had been waiting for her when she came out of the bathing unit. "There could be problems with the colony, and we need someone who can protect you should the need arise."

Of course, there were going to be problems. The Keagans, especially the elder, were used to getting their own way. There was no way Boyd was going to let her go without a fight. "I guess I hadn't thought about it."

Never really comfortable with dressing in front of others, Libby turned away and slipped on her shirt and pants. "What about your brother? Is he going to be okay with this?" Would he end up in a fight if another male showed up at his home unexpectedly? What she really wanted to know was whether or not he'd offer to claim her himself. The answer to that was a huge "no." If he wanted to help— wanted her—he would already have asked.

"Do not worry. It is taken care of."

This was her future they were discussing. How could she *not* worry?

CHAPTER EIGHT

Knowing the level of Nyssa's determination, Erak had been surprised she hadn't argued when he'd refused to allow Libby to accompany her to the bar. Until she was claimed, it would be difficult protecting the gorgeous female from numerous interested males. He didn't want anyone else to claim her, his real reason for not letting her go.

Libby had been silent during their entire trip to his dwelling, no doubt because she was still angry at him. He'd assumed she would reject his offer to prepare her an evening meal, preferring to avoid him completely. Not only had she accepted, but she'd helped him with the preparation.

She hadn't spoken much since they'd returned from the command facility. Sharing the meal had been quiet and comfortable, no tension between them. Once they finished, he pushed his chair away from the table and set their empty plates on the counter. He reached into an overhead storage area for a small container, then filled it with the remaining berries and sliced fruit from the serving bowl.

"Anything I can help with?" Libby asked, walking around to the opposite side of the counter.

"No, almost done."

He couldn't help admiring how well the simple yet traditional soft blue Tarron gown she wore accented the curves of her petite frame. "You are very beautiful. The dress suits you. My sister did well in selecting a wardrobe for you."

"Thank you." She smiled, a flush rising on her cheeks. "I think she bought more than was necessary. As soon as I'm settled, wherever that may be, I plan to repay you for your generosity."

He reached across the counter and took her hand. "I do not expect to be compensated. They are a gift."

"But…"

"Please, it would honor me for you to accept."

"Since you said please, how could I refuse," Libby teased.

If she belonged to him, he would give her more than a few items of clothing. Along with his possessive thought came the reminder of Keagan and the threat he posed to her. He pulled her around the counter, intent on giving her one evening where she wasn't reminded of her troubling situation. "Would you mind taking a walk with me? There is something I would like to show you."

"Sure."

Holding the container in one hand, he continued holding hers with the other and took her to the property behind his home. The day was slowly fading into night, but there was still enough sunlight left to see where they were going.

"What's the fruit for?"

"You will see." He led her along a path that curved its way through a thick wall of trees. At the end of the trail was a clearing bordered by a stream on one side and a low wall of boulders on the other.

"Come, sit here." He made room for her next to him on the flat area of a low rock formation.

She climbed up next to him, slowly glancing at the surrounding landscape.

"It is my favorite spot." One of the reasons he'd chosen the secluded area to build his home.

"This place is wonderful. I can see why you like it," she said.

"I come here when I am stressed and need to relax."

"You, stressed? Never." Libby's contagious laugh filled the air.

Erak realized she was teasing him, and chuckled. "I know it is hard to believe since I am so calm and easygoing." He slapped his hand against his chest, feigning innocence.

When they both stopped laughing, he took her hand and held her gaze. "I have never brought anyone here before." He hadn't even shown his secret place to Sharra. Though, now that he thought about it, Erak doubted the selfish woman would have appreciated the rare beauty and tranquility the place had to offer. Not like Libby, who seemed to enjoy it the same way he did.

Libby cared about things that were important. She didn't seem to crave the things only status and power provided. He'd witnessed the depths of her concern aboard the Klorthon's vessel. First when she'd put her life at risk to save his, then later when she nursed his wounds, and cared for the female called Britta.

His. Synge had referred to Libby as "his female." Could she belong to him? Did she belong to him?

"It really is amazing. Thank you for sharing it with me." She glanced at the container he'd placed on his other side. "Are you planning to spend the night out here? Is that why you brought the fruit? In case you get hungry?"

Sliding off the rock, he opened the container and set it on the ground near an overgrowth of thorny hedges. He returned to his seat. "I brought it for them."

"Them?" she asked.

"Watch."

A few seconds later, the branches of the hedge rustled. Two little animals with mustard-colored oval eyes peeked out from beneath the lower leaves. One eased farther into the clearing. Short and spiky deep-purple fur covered its entire body. It sniffed the air and glanced in their direction, then cautiously approached the container.

"They're so cute. Kind of like foxes back on Earth. Only with much bigger claws and a shorter tail. What are they?" Libby asked.

"Brigatreils." One of the creatures flipped the container on its side and snatched a berry. A few seconds later, the other one joined the first, helping itself to the spilled fruit.

"Are they dangerous?" She didn't seem afraid, only curious.

Erak pointed to the scar running along his index finger. "Only if you get too close while they are eating."

"No petting, then." Libby pretended to pout.

"I am afraid not."

"Does anything else live out here?"

"Nothing that I have found on my entire property."

"You own all this?" she asked.

"Yes. Does this shock you?"

"It seems like a lot for one person."

"When I purchased it, I had one day hoped to have a family." He tamped down the longing associated with his unfulfilled dream. "Things did not work out as I had planned."

"I didn't mean to pry."

He placed her hand on his thigh, entwining his fingers through hers. "It was a long time ago."

"I assume there was a woman?"

"Yes." He was astonished by her perception and how easy it was to open up to her.

"What was her name?" She squeezed his hand. "You won't hurt my feelings if you don't want to talk about it."

"Sharra." Surprisingly, saying her name out loud no longer hurt the way it had in the past. "I chose her as my mate and offered to claim her. She refused me for another, someone who granted her a higher status with more wealth and power."

Libby placed her other hand on his arm. "I'm so sorry."

"Do not be sorry. If she had been my true mate, nothing would have prevented our joining."

"I don't understand. What's a true mate?" Libby asked.

"For every Tarron male, there is the perfect female. The one that is his match and meant to join with him for the entirety of his life."

"Are Ricka and Synge true mates?"

"Yes, they were very lucky to find each other. Not everyone finds the person they are meant to be with. Many of my people settle, choosing to mate for different reasons."

"If a claiming is similar to an engagement, and can be broken, what's a joining?"

"It is a vow of belonging and commitment the couple makes to each other," Erak said.

"Is it permanent?"

"Yes. Unlike the human marriage, once made, it cannot be broken."

#

When Libby had first arrived in the city, she'd sensed Erak

might be hiding a deep hurt, and she'd been right. She wondered how much the rejection had played a part in his reluctance to accept being assigned to protect her by the commander. The more time she spent with him, the more she liked him. Underneath his moody and abrasive demeanor was an honorable and caring man. As far as she was concerned, this Sharra person hadn't deserved him.

She already cared about him more than she should. If she wasn't careful, he might find his way into her heart. Who was she kidding? He already had. A very bad thing since she was running out of time and needed to accept the claim of another to escape Boyd. She had a feeling once her decision was made, she'd probably never see Erak again.

Libby watched the pair of brigatreils finish off the last of the fruit before disappearing into the unusual hedge-like plant with two-inch thorns.

Erak pushed off the rock, picked up the container, then offered her his hand. "We should be getting back. The last of the light will be gone soon, and walking will be difficult."

"I thought you could see in the dark." During her visit with Ricka, she'd learned the Tarrons had heightened senses, which included their sight and sense of smell.

"I can, but you cannot. I would be more than happy to carry you back if you would like to stay longer." He flashed her a devilish grin.

Damn, the man had a gorgeous smile when he chose to use it. "I appreciate the offer, but it won't be necessary. We can go back now." Her body had experienced high heat levels the last time he held her in his arms. Being snuggled up against his chest would probably send her up in flames. If she let him carry her, she wouldn't want him to set her back down.

The tranquil feeling of safety and belonging she'd come to associate with his nearness enveloped her. They fell into a comfortable silence during their return walk.

Erak swiped his hand over the sensor, triggering the rear-door panel. As soon as they were inside, he set the container on a nearby table and pulled her into his arms. "I have been waiting all day to do this." His mouth covered hers, his kiss possessive and urgent.

Warmth spread to her core, stealing her ability for rational thought. He held her as if she were the last morsel of food on the planet and he would starve without her. She ran her hands along his chest, palming his sculpted muscles, reaching for his broad shoulders.

Splaying his hand across her back, he pulled her closer. He tangled his fingers in her hair and angled her head. She moaned, parting her lips so he could explore her mouth more thoroughly. Erak ignited something inside her, a part of her that sought only him. Even Trey, with all his thoughtfulness and caring, hadn't sparked the desire burning through her. All the reasons she'd listed for this being a bad idea dissolved. She wanted him, needed him, even if it was only for tonight.

"Where have you two been?" Nyssa's words were slightly slurred.

The overhead lights sprang to life, illuminating the room, startling Libby. Her already flushed cheeks grew hotter.

Erak's irritated growl vibrated against her. He shot his sister a deadly glare and slowly released Libby. "What are you doing here? Can't you stay at your own home?"

Nyssa staggered toward the closest chair, then perched her ass on the edge. She held the frame in a death grip as if she was afraid she might suddenly slide to the floor. It was apparent she'd had a bit too much to drink.

"We have already discussed this. Our parents will not be back for a few weeks, and I am still avoiding Bokar. Besides, I wanted to make sure Libby was all right," Nyssa said.

"She is perfectly fine. I would never hurt her."

Nyssa laughed. "I was more afraid she might want to strangle your cranky ass."

"Why do you persist in telling everyone that I am cranky?"

Nyssa snorted. "Maybe because you are."

Right now, it wasn't Erak she wanted to strangle. It was his sister. Libby knew she should be grateful. She wasn't the type of woman to settle for one night of great sex. And that was what it would have been. Erak might have protested against his sister's plan to find someone to claim her, but he hadn't offered to take on the responsibility himself.

It was better this way. Safer. Especially for her heart.

Seeing where the discussion was going, Libby shook her head and stepped between the two. "Your brother was the perfect host. Believe it or not, he even smiled."

Nyssa smirked. "I cannot believe I missed it."

Libby was afraid his sister, in her inebriated state, might want to discuss "the plan" in front of Erak. She didn't want to ruin the memory of the wonderful evening she'd spent with him, or the intoxicating kiss they'd shared. Instead of facing the inevitable, she pressed her hands against his chest. "I'm exhausted, so I think I'll head to bed." Standing on her tiptoes, she placed a soft kiss on his cheek. "Thank you…for everything."

Holding back the tears threatening to fall, she hastened for the stairs. Damn her aching heart. Tomorrow, her life was going to change. Forever. And he'd no longer be a part of it.

#

Erak woke with the first rays of sunlight from a limited night of sleep. Part of the time he'd spent in sexual frustration fighting the impulse to throttle his interfering sister. The remainder, disturbed by the parting words Libby had spoken right before she'd kissed him on the cheek, then left to go to her room. He couldn't shake the feeling the good-bye had meant something more.

He could no longer deny that Libby belonged to him. She'd found a way into his heart, and he'd be damned if he was going to let her leave. After realizing how much he cared for her, needed her, he'd devised a plan to make sure she stayed with him. He would offer his claim, or insist, if she tried to refuse.

Boyd was a determined asshole, and there was a good chance he would continually check on Libby to ensure the claim was not a ruse to keep her away from him. It meant she would have to stay with Erak for an extended length of time. Time he planned to use to his advantage and convince her to be his mate. Erak feared the thought of losing her more than he did her possible rejection. If he was unable to convince her to be his, her refusal would destroy him, but it was now a risk he was willing to take.

Erak quickly showered and dressed, then headed for the lower level. He'd been determined to get Libby alone but didn't get the chance. Nyssa, who never started any day early, ever, was up preparing a meal and wouldn't leave Libby's side.

Shortly after they'd eaten, Synge arrived with Ricka. His female had brought Earth virtuals of something she called "chick flicks." According to the three women, they planned to have something called a girl-bonding day, and neither male was invited. After they made numerous assurances they would not leave the house, he reluctantly left with his friend to spend the remainder of the day at command headquarters.

To add to his increasing aggravation, he'd received a transmission from the team searching for Larn and Balok. The lead they had tracked down had been worthless. The location had been abandoned by the time they'd arrived. They were no closer to finding his friends or the fighting arenas. He feared they might already have run out of time.

Midway through the afternoon, Ryos walked into his office, his expression more serious and grim than usual. "Do you have a moment?"

Erak pushed away from the control display and got to his feet. "Of course."

"I received word from Boyd Keagan. The colony ship will be arriving tomorrow."

"He was not supposed to arrive for several more days." Erak rubbed the tension building at the base of his neck.

"Apparently, he is in a hurry to retrieve the female."

"We cannot let him take Libby."

"You know there is nothing I can do. I am bound by *all* the laws. Have her here in the morning when he arrives." Ryos turned and left the room.

Can things possibly get any worse? Keagan was never going to get his hands on Libby. He needed to get his ass home. Erak didn't care if she was in the middle of some kind of girl-bonding thing or not, he was going to claim her. First, he had to find Synge. He never should have let his friend talk him into riding with him and leaving his transport at his home.

He stormed out of the room and was halfway down the hall when he spotted Kel heading toward him. "Synge left early to pick up Ricka." He held up his hand. "And before you get upset, I have been instructed to inform you Nyssa and Libby are still at your home. I am your ride, so let me know when you are ready to leave."

"Now," Erak growled. "I am ready to go *now*."

Kel nodded, then remained silent until they were seated inside his vehicle. "I sense something is troubling you, my friend. Let me buy you a drink. I would hate for you to lose your temper, or do something you might regret. Especially in front of your female houseguest."

Sometimes he hated that Kel understood him so well. He was one of the few friends who knew about Sharra and had helped him deal with her rejection. As determined as he was to claim Libby, he didn't want to be angry when he asked her. "Fine. One drink, then you take me home."

"Agreed," Kel said.

Kel took him to their favorite bar located close to the command facility. Hunters and city dwellers frequented the establishment. Luckily, it was early and not very crowded. Erak recognized a couple of the males seated at one of the tables. He tipped his head in their direction as he followed Kel to some stools at the secluded end of the bar.

The bartender, a Tarron female, strolled over to them. Propping her elbows on the counter, she leaned forward, exposing an ample view of her cleavage. "What can I get for you, handsome?" She smiled at Erak, an unspoken invitation in her light-golden gaze.

Kel winked. "I know what you can get for me, or better yet do for me."

Kel was a master of seduction with a reputation to go along with the title. Erak knew it wouldn't take his flirtatious friend long to get the female into his bed. Something he had no interest in watching, not when getting home to Libby was all that mattered. "Two drevas," he grumbled.

"Sure." The woman frowned and went to retrieve their drinks.

"You, my friend, are no fun." Kel stared longingly after the female.

Erak snorted, "On that we agree."

"Would you like to tell me what is going on?" Kel shifted slightly, giving Erak his full attention. "Does this have something to do with your human female?"

Erak suspiciously studied him. "Why would you make that assumption?"

"I know Nyssa is staying with you. She irritates you daily, and it never makes you this irritable."

The bartender returned with two tall glasses filled with a dark blue liquid. Ignoring Erak, she smiled at Kel. "Let me know if you need anything else." She walked away to take care of another customer.

"Very promising." Kel grinned and took a sip of his drink.

Erak groaned and gripped the base of his glass. "How much do you know about Libby's situation?"

"I heard Keagan's nephew plans to take her as a bride and will be arriving from the colony within a few days. Why?"

"The commander informed me his ship will be here in the morning," Erak said.

"You will finally be rid of her, so what is the problem?"

"She deserves much better than that asshole."

Kel downed the rest of his drink. "If that is all you are worried about, you can relax. Nyssa found someone to claim your female. He should be arriving at your home anytime now to formalize the paperwork." Kel rubbed his chin. "If he changes his mind, I already told your sister I would be willing to help. The human female is very attractive. You know I am not much for settling down or finding a mate, but spending a few months between those lovely legs might be worth it."

Erak's chest tightened, his temper threatening to explode. He gripped his glass tighter to keep from punching his friend. "What? When did you talk to Nyssa?"

"Yesterday. Did she not tell you?"

Fuck, I am going to kill her. "No," Erak growled loud enough to turn a few heads. Libby must have known what his sister had planned. Yet she'd responded to his kisses, melted in his arms. Her sad expression, the words of good-bye. Damn, he'd been such an idiot. He hadn't claimed her, so she was going to accept someone else's offer. "You will not touch her. She belongs to me." He drained the contents of his glass, then slammed it on the counter. "I am taking your transport." He slid off the stool and stormed for the exit.

CHAPTER NINE

Nyssa stood in the gathering room of Erak's home, patiently waiting for the next part of her plan to be executed. She'd barely tolerated Sharra and hated the superficial female for what she'd done to Erak. The bitch had refused his claim and chosen another Tarron with more status.

Erak never talked about it, but the woman's rejection had changed him, broken something inside, and he'd never been the same. The outgoing male she'd grown up with became the moody, reserved man he was now. Then Libby came along, and Nyssa had noticed something spark to life again inside her brother.

There was definitely chemistry between them. Anyone who spent any time with them could see it in the way they looked at each other. The more she observed them, the more she was convinced they were true mates. It was one of the reasons she'd devised her scheme, devious as it was. She really liked the thoughtful, caring human and hated the idea of the colony male forcing her new friend into a life of sexual servitude.

Besides, what kind of sister would she be if she didn't do everything possible to guarantee her brother's happiness?

Her well-designed plan had almost been ruined by Lyna's challenge to try an exotic and extremely potent ale. For a human, the female could definitely outdrink most Tarron males. Luckily, Dathan's arrival at the bar had distracted her long enough for Nyssa to leave. She'd arrived at Erak's home the night before in time to stop him from seducing Libby.

Because of her brother's vow to remain unmated, she'd been afraid if they'd had sex, Erak would still shy away from claiming the sweet female. Keeping them apart had been necessary to ensure the success of the next and final step.

Nyssa had silently cursed herself when she'd arrived and found the couple one step away from heading to the bedroom. Even with her head throbbing and inability to remain standing for any length of time, she'd been prepared to do whatever it took to keep the couple apart. Thankfully, Libby had made it easy by retiring early.

Her communicator beeped, and she glanced at the message, grinning. *"Erak extremely pissed and heading home."* As promised, Kel had lured her brother out for drinks, then did what he did best. He teased and irritated Erak until he was close to losing his temper. Unless her brother found a way to make the transport fly—totally possible—it would be awhile before he arrived.

She truly loved their loyal friends. It had taken quite a bit of convincing, but all of them, including Synge and Ricka, offered their help in bringing the two together. Ryos, whom she'd known since she was a child, had secretly conspired to assist.

An intermittent beep rang through the gathering room, alerting her to someone's arrival. *Perfect timing.* The final part of her plan was right on schedule. She waved her hand over the sensor, opening the front door.

Dathan stepped inside. He seemed uncomfortable holding a bouquet of blossoms. "Tell me again why I needed to bring these smelly things?"

"Supposedly it is an Earth custom. Human females like receiving flowers." Glaring at him, she tugged him toward the gathering room. "And keep your voice down. Libby cannot know what we are doing."

He glanced around the room. "Where is she anyway? Kel said she is quite beautiful. If Erak does not want her, maybe I will…"

"In the bedroom getting ready." Nyssa punched him in the shoulder. "Stick to the plan, and do not even think about it. She is my brother's true mate, and I will not let anyone screw this up for him."

"All right, all right. No need to get violent." Dathan sighed and walked farther into the room. "Are you sure this is going to work?"

Unless my brother does something stupid. "Of course, I am sure."

He rubbed the back of his head. "I still have the scar from the last time one of your schemes did not work and your uptight brother lost his temper."

Nyssa rolled her eyes. "Stop being so dramatic. It will work. I promise." She headed for the stairs. "Stay here. I will go see if she is ready."

#

Nyssa stuck her head through the open doorway to Libby's bedroom. "Dathan is here. Are you ready?"

Not really. "I guess so." Libby stepped away from the mirror and nervously swiped her hands down the front of the shimmering blue dress Nyssa had purchased for her. She didn't think she'd ever get used to the clothes worn by Tarron women. Everything had a low-cut neckline and was designed to show off large portions of skin on their abdomens. At least the length reached her mid-thigh and she didn't have to worry about her ass being exposed.

"You look wonderful," Nyssa said.

A knot stiffened in Libby's belly. "I don't think I can do this."

"Of course you can. Do not worry. Remember, this is only temporary. You only have to live with him for a few months, then you can have the claiming dissolved."

"But what if he expects, you know…sex."

"Even if he finds you attractive, he has assured me it will not be an issue." Nyssa placed a comforting hand on Libby's arm. "I have known him for years. He is an honorable man and a good friend. He only wants to help and will take good care of you."

Nyssa frowned. "You have not changed your mind about marrying the colony asshole, have you?"

The knot, compounded by the thought of being stuck with Boyd for the rest of her life, grew much larger. "No, I haven't changed my mind. It's…"

Understanding reflected in Nyssa's golden gaze. "You wish it were my brother."

"Yes." Libby groaned. "Is it that obvious?"

"To everyone but him."

The kisses she'd shared with Erak had been so powerful and

passionate. He'd been kind, compassionate, and Libby had fallen in love with him. It was breaking her heart to think he didn't care about her the same way. She had to accept the facts. He'd known what was going to happen to her, and yet he hadn't offered to claim her. "I think Sharra hurt him too deeply."

"He told you about her?" Nyssa asked, surprised.

Libby nodded. "Last night."

"He never talks about her with anyone, not even me. Please do not be sad. Things have a way of working themselves out."

"I'm sure you're right." Libby wished she could believe her. "I wanted to thank you."

"For what?" Nyssa asked.

"For trying to help, and for being a good friend."

"You are most welcome." Nyssa took her hand. "Come. We should not keep Dathan waiting any longer."

#

Erak stormed into the house, his mood only mildly less irritated than when he'd left Kel at the bar. It had taken every ounce of his reserve not to punch him in the jaw before he left. Dammit, the man was supposed to be his friend. Yet he had no problem expressing his desire to bed Libby. The female Erak loved. The female who was going to be his mate.

He froze when he saw Libby standing next to his sister in the middle of the gathering room. She wore an elegant Tarron gown, a lustrous shade of blue that enhanced the color of her eyes. Her golden locks were curled more than usual, the shiny spirals begging to be touched. His gaze locked on her shocked expression. He couldn't move, couldn't breathe, couldn't speak. All he could do was stare at the entrancing female who'd stolen his heart.

"What are you doing here?" Nyssa asked, sounding as if he'd walked in and found her kissing a male friend.

"I live here, remember?" Erak snapped, then noticed Dathan standing off to the side, holding a bunch of blossoms. "Why is he here? And what are those for?"

"I have come to submit a claim. These are for her, a customary Earth courting gift, I believe."

Erak glared at his friend, irritated that he had the audacity to appear amused. He turned his attention back to his sister. "You asked *him* to claim Libby?"

"He has come to help. No one wants her to be handed over to that Rivean sheraaat." She gave Libby a sympathetic glance and squeezed her hand. "I would have asked Synge, but he is already taken. Dathan is the only other person I trust to take care of her." Nyssa tapped her lips. "I suppose if she does not like him, I could always ask Kel. He seemed to *really* like her, but he has such a bad reputation with the females, I thought this would be much safer."

Dathan furrowed his brows. "Thank you for the low opinion of my prowess."

Nyssa snorted. "Anytime."

Joking at a time like this. Are they serious? He glanced from one to the other, not sure who had angered him more. "Did it not occur to you to ask me to help?"

"No," Dathan and Nyssa answered at the same time.

"What?" He couldn't believe what he was hearing. "Why?"

"Ricka told me about your displeasure at being assigned to escort Libby. Then there is the fact that you avoid relationships and have made it clear you will not ever take a mate." Empathy flashed across his sister's features, and she softened her tone. "I know how badly you have been hurt and did not want to add to your pain."

Scheming and devious as she was, his sister had always cared about him. Did what she thought was best for him. "I appreciate your concern, but his offer will not be necessary."

"Why not?" Dathan sounded disappointed and lowered the bouquet of blossoms to his side.

Erak had no intention of explaining himself to his friend. "I need you both to leave. *Now.*"

"Are you sure?" Dathan asked.

"Yes." He held Libby's confused gaze. "Please escort my sister to our parents' home."

"We cannot leave her. The claim has not yet been finalized," Nyssa argued.

"No further discussion is needed. I am not incapable of seeing to her needs. Now go before I lose my temper."

"I am sure the female will be fine, and I do not wish to sustain any unnecessary injuries." Dathan snatched Nyssa's wrist.

"We are leaving."

Nyssa glanced over her shoulder at Libby. "If you need anything, anything at all, you know how to contact me."

"She will not require your assistance." Erak stalked to the front entrance and activated the sensor to open the door. "Go."

CHAPTER TEN

When Erak burst into the room, Libby's heart plummeted to her stomach. His face held a mixture of emotions. First anger and hurt, then desire. She wanted to say something, to go to him, to take him in her arms. Nyssa had gripped her hand firmly and, with a slight shake of her head, had signaled her to stay where she was and remain silent.

Libby waited to see what he'd do, and asking them to leave was the last thing she'd expected. The door closed with a snap, and she jumped.

His intense gaze locked on her, never wavering as he slowly removed his weapon holster and set it on the nearest chair. Using the same stealthy stride she'd witnessed the day before, he approached her, not stopping until they were inches apart and he'd nearly consumed her space. He brushed his thumb along her jaw, causing her to shudder. "No one will be claiming you but me."

He pulled her into his arms and captured her lips, his kiss demanding, taking what he wanted, removing any doubts that he planned to make her his. Her heart raced, her body warmed to an abnormally high level. She didn't care that he wasn't asking or giving her a choice. All she wanted, all she needed, was to surrender to the man who had enslaved her heart.

Melting into him, she eagerly took what he had to offer. She moved her hands along his chest, encircling his neck. He slid his hand to her lower back, pressing her closer. She moaned and rubbed against his erection.

Erak loosened his hold long enough to scoop her in his arms and carry her to his room. Once inside, he gently lowered her to her feet, keeping one arm braced around her waist. "You are mine, and I will never give you up."

He traced a fingertip along her chest, then moved to her nape to undo the only tie holding the dress in place. He pushed the fabric to the floor, removing her underwear along with it. Once she was completely naked, he took a step back, and murmured, "So damned beautiful."

Her entire body ignited under his perusal. Taking a step back, he toed off his boots, then undid the fastenings on his shirt, quickly stripping off the rest of his clothes and tossing them on the floor. Libby stared; she couldn't help it. He was every bit as firm and muscular below the waist as he was above it. Other than his erection being larger and thicker, it didn't appear to be much different from a human.

"Do you approve?" he asked, raising an eyebrow.

She snapped her head up, embarrassed. "I...yes." What else could she say after he'd caught her gawking with her mouth open.

Placing his hands on her hips, he tugged her forward, then brushed his lips tenderly across hers. He nuzzled her neck, trailing hot kisses along her throat. "You belong to me, and I am going to make you mine."

Heat rolled through her, and she trembled, enflamed by the prospect. She pressed her hands against the firm muscles of his chest. Using her fingertips, she traced the path of unusual markings along his left side and down his abdomen. A groan escaped his lips, and he shuddered beneath her touch. She smiled, remembering their time on the Klorthons' vessel when she'd run her fingers across his shoulder and gotten a similar reaction.

Erak was always so controlled and guarded with his emotions. It was exhilarating to know she could elicit such a passionate response with a simple touch.

Her explorations were cut short when he sought her lips again, his actions greedy and relentless. He inched his hand slowly along her ribs, burning a path to her breast. One squeeze from his warm hand, and heat slammed through her. Her body thrummed with need, and she ground her hips against him. The craving to have him inside her was like nothing she'd ever felt before. "Please..."

Lifting her off the ground, he carried her to the bed. Laying her on her back, he covered her with his body, his hips fitting perfectly between her spread legs. He grinned wickedly and pressed kisses along her stomach as he slowly worked his way upward.

"Oh God," Libby whimpered and writhed beneath him, not sure how much more of his exquisite torture she'd be able to survive.

He sucked a breast into his mouth, and swirled his tongue around the nipple. It hardened immediately, shooting straight to her core. He switched to her other breast, giving it the same attention. His tongue was like magic, stoking her arousal.

She ran her hands along his arms, his shoulders, aching to touch every part of him she could reach. On some primal level, she knew he belonged to her, and she wanted to possess him as much as he was possessing her.

He released her breast, then used those wonderful lips to place kisses along her throat, steadily moving upward until he hovered inches from her face. "Look at me." His tone was low, deep, seductive.

Libby struggled with rational thought as she focused her attention on his handsome features. His hungry gaze had darkened to the most extraordinary shade of amber she'd ever seen. Taking her wrists, he gently but firmly placed them on the bed above her head. He ran his other hand along her inner thigh. "Tell me you accept me, that you belong to me." Sliding two fingers inside her, he slowly pumped in and out, driving her need even higher.

"Oh God." She pressed into him, wanting him, needing him.

"Tell me."

"I belong to you." There was no doubt, no hesitation. Somehow she'd known they were meant to be together from the moment they'd met.

He withdrew his hand and adjusted his hips, pushing into her slowly. She spread her legs wider, more than ready to accept his large size. He pulled back and thrust, gradually repeating the motion and building into a steady rhythm. She gasped, arching into him, digging her nails into his back, straining for release.

"Oh my...I'm—" Her climax hit, and she shattered with a pleasure so intense, she feared blacking out. He increased his pace, his thrusts faster, stronger. He growled, surging a final time within her, seeking his own release. He collapsed on top of her, bracing his arms to keep from crushing her. After their breathing returned to normal, he rolled on his back, hauling her with him.

Libby curled against his side, draping her leg across his thighs and nestling her head on his shoulder.

"Rest." He twirled a lock of her hair around his finger. "I have not finished with you yet."

But even though the prospect of more amazing sex with Erak thrilled her, she couldn't shake Boyd's threat from her mind. It slithered through her thoughts like a deadly snake ready to strike. He'd been too determined to have her. Would he really accept the claiming and walk away without a fight?

#

Erak woke to find Libby still asleep and tucked against him, her hand splayed on his chest. He pushed the hair off her cheek, brushing his knuckles against her creamy skin. A small smile tugged on her lovely lips, and she snuggled closer. "Can we stay like this for the rest of the day?"

He'd found his true mate, had known it the instant their bodies had joined. Libby might not be aware of the connection yet, so he planned to give her some time before taking her to one of the arreinian pools. Saying their vows of bonding in the sacred waters of his people was the final act of the joining process.

They'd already completed the first part of the ritual when they'd professed the words of belonging to each other.

The only hurdle standing in their way was Keagan. He hated to ruin her day, but he couldn't put off telling her any longer. "I am afraid not. We need to file the claiming documents before Boyd arrives this morning."

Her eyes flew open, and she stiffened against him. "He's here? Why didn't you tell me?"

"I did not want to upset you and feared you would assume it was the reason I claimed you."

"What if he refuses to accept the claiming, and tries to force me to go with him?"

Erak hated the human male even more for causing the worry in her gaze. "It will not matter. He has no jurisdiction on Tarron, and I will not allow him to get near you."

He felt some of the tension ease from her body. She bit her lower lip and lightly stroked the markings along his shoulder. "Why did you claim me?"

He ran his thumb along her chin. "Because, my beautiful mate, I love you and want to join with you."

"That's a good thing, because I love you too."

He thought his heart might explode. Dipping his head, he gave her a tender kiss. Finally, and a little grudgingly, he released her. Rolling off the bed, he held out his hand. "Come, I think we have enough time for me to give you a proper cleaning."

"What exactly does that entail?"

Gripping her ass, he hoisted her off the floor. She squealed, grabbed for his neck, and wrapped her legs around his waist.

"I will be more than happy to demonstrate." He grinned and headed for the bathing unit.

#

Erak stopped Libby in the hall outside the commander's waiting room and office. "Your hand is shaking? Are you all right?" He wrapped his arms around her waist, knowing Keagan was the cause of her discomfort.

She took a deep breath. "A little nervous, I guess."

"This is a formality. The colony will require verification of the claiming." Completing the document was for the human's benefit. No one on Tarron would dispute his claim to Libby.

"I understand." She gave him a weak smile.

"If it were my choice, I would not allow him in the same room with you. I will be with you the entire time. He will not get near you, I promise." He pressed a kiss to her forehead. "You have not changed your mind, have you?"

"No. Never."

Several hunters walked by, nodding at him as they passed. Erak nuzzled her neck, speaking so low, only she could hear him. "As much as I regret not being able to spend more time and skills convincing you, I am glad to hear it."

"Maybe when we get home, you can explain in more detail what kind of skills you would be willing to use." She grinned and leaned into him. "In case I have any lingering doubts."

"Temptress," he hissed, an erection pressing uncomfortably against the fabric of his pants.

"Temptress, really?" She slid her hands to his shoulders. "Where did you learn that word?"

"Do not sound so surprised. I do have a knowledge of Earth sayings."

She eyed him skeptically. "Uh-huh."

"Fine. I borrowed one of my sister's virtuals." He stepped away and took her hand. "We need to go inside, unless you want me to…oh yes, ravage you right here."

Libby giggled. "I am definitely confiscating those virtuals."

Libby sat in a chair opposite the commander's desk. Erak took a position behind her. He preferred to stand in case things went badly with Keagan and he needed to access his weapon quickly.

Ryos set the paperwork in front of him, then directed his gaze to Libby. "Before I complete the agreement, I need to know if you were forced in any way to sign this document."

Erak's body stiffened, and he dug his nails into the back of her chair. "What? Sir, I would never…"

Ryos held up his hand. "Do not take offense. Know that I am only asking in case the question arises later in a conversation with the colony officials. It is quite apparent you two are well suited."

Libby glanced at him over her shoulder and gave him a confident smile. "No, I wasn't forced. I accept this claiming with all my heart." Her expressive and caring words soothed his irritation.

"Then you have my congratulations. I am happy for both of you." Ryos finalized the document with his signature. "You know Keagan will not be happy about this. He is sure to cause problems."

"I assumed as much." Erak placed a comforting hand on Libby's tense shoulder. "I have asked Kel and Torin to remain nearby in case we require assistance."

The communicator in the display panel on the commander's desk beeped, then blinked bright green.

Ryos tapped a button. "Yes."

"Sir, the escorts have arrived with the human male you were expecting." His assistant's harsh voice sounded from the comlink.

"Are you ready?" Ryos asked.

She rose from her seat and stood next to Erak. "Yes."

"Send him in." Ryos tapped another button to disconnect the transmission.

Seconds later, the door slid open, and Boyd strode into the room like he owned the place. The human barely resembled the freshly polished male Erak had seen on the virtucom days ago. Facial hair lined the jaw of his haggard face, his dark eyes narrowed and wary. His worn and wrinkled clothes looked like they'd been slept in for several days.

"Would you like to take a seat?" Ryos asked, pointing to the chair Libby had vacated.

"No, I don't plan on being here very long." Boyd focused his attention on Erak's mate. "Hello, Libby." He licked his lips, scrutinizing her from top to bottom as if appreciating a piece of valuable property. "You're even better looking than the last time I saw you. I can't wait to get you back to my ship so we can get to know each other better."

Erak fought the urge to rip the male's throat out. Instead, he took a step forward to block her from his view.

Boyd puffed out his chest and glared at him. "I appreciate you taking care of my future wife, but if you don't mind, I'd like to take her and get out of here."

"I am afraid the female will not be leaving with you," Ryos said.

"What the hell are you talking about? You can't keep her here." Spots of red mottled Boyd's cheeks. "I have a contract that says she has to come with me." Boyd leaned forward, slamming his hands on the edge of the desk. "My uncle will not be happy to hear that you are detaining a colony citizen."

"She is not being kept here against her will." Ryos slowly rose to his feet. His intimidating and towering stance forced Boyd to take a step back. "She has willingly accepted a claim and is officially a Tarron resident."

"What do you mean claimed, and by who?"

"By me." Erak placed a protective arm around her waist. "I am her mate."

"This is bullshit. You can't keep her away from me." Boyd's arms stiffened, his hands balled into fists. "Your claims mean nothing. She has to abide by the terms of her contract, which means I own her."

"You no longer have any rights where she is concerned. I have reviewed the agreement. It clearly states the female can be released from her obligation with the mining corporation if she can provide documentation of another commitment." Ryos set the recently executed claiming document on the desk in front of Boyd. "Per Tarron law, claiming a mate is the equivalent to such a commitment."

Ryos waved a hand toward the entrance. "I have made arrangements for you to be returned to your vessel." As if on cue, the door slid open and two guards appeared. "Please accept my apologies. I am sorry your trip here was wasted. These men will see you safely back to your ship."

Boyd glanced at the piece of paper, then glared at the commander. "This isn't over." He shoved past his escort and stormed out of the office.

Ryos returned to his seat. "That went better than I anticipated."

Erak had been prepared for a show of force. "Even so, I do not trust the human.

"Do you think he will try something?" Libby leaned into him.

"I will have someone keep a close surveillance on his ship until they launch. In the meantime, make sure you take precautions to protect your female."

CHAPTER ELEVEN

Libby stood in front of the virtucom located in the upper level of Erak's home. Now her home. A fact she still had a hard time believing.

She tapped a button on the control panel, and Ricka's image filled the screen. Her friend had contacted her during the trip to hunter command. Apparently, Synge had informed his mate about Boyd's arrival. Ricka had been upset and wanted to be there when he arrived. Knowing her friend's overprotective nature, Libby had refused the support and promised to check in after the meeting. "Hey."

"Hey, back. How are you doing?" Ricka asked.

"A lot better now. I'm glad it's over, and I don't have to go back to Rivean."

"How did Boyd take the news?"

"He was pretty upset." Upset was the mild way of saying Boyd had been on the verge of snapping. Libby rubbed her arms, trying to push the memory of his volatile reaction from her mind. "I think he was too afraid of the commander to start anything."

"Yeah, he can be scary and intimidating." Ricka chuckled. "I'm sorry I didn't get to threaten him with my knife."

Libby groaned. "Please tell me Synge didn't actually give that darned thing back to you."

"No, not yet, but he will."

Libby recognized the determined look and decided not to ask. Sometimes with Ricka, it was better not knowing.

"How are things going with Erak? I can't believe he finally came to his senses and claimed you. Though, at first, I had my doubts and was worried he might break your heart," Ricka said.

"Why would you think he…"

"Unless they're a complete fool, anyone spending five seconds around you two couldn't miss the attraction."

"Oh," Libby said.

"So, how was the sex?" Ricka asked.

"Who says…and why would you ask me that?" Libby nearly choked.

"Tarron males have a voracious sexual appetite. I was curious. They say it's the quiet and moody ones who are wild in the bedroom." Ricka wiggled her eyebrows. "Going by the nice blush on your cheeks, I'd say I have my answer. Good for you."

"Should I be asking you the same thing about your…" Libby made quote marks with her fingers. "Bodacious hunk?"

"Definitely no complaints." Ricka propped her chin on her elbows. "Now that you are claimed, you won't be confined to staying in the city. We're going home tomorrow. Why don't you both come out and spend a couple of days with us?"

"I'd like that. I'll ask Erak when he gets back home."

"So where is your cranky mate?"

"He's not…never mind. There was some kind of emergency with an important visitor he had to take care of."

"What? He left you alone with Boyd still in the city?" Concern flashed across Ricka's expression. "I don't trust that asshole. Maybe Synge and I should come stay with you until he returns."

"I'll be fine. He sent Kel along to protect me."

"Seriously? He left you alone with the dangerous flirt whose main goal in life is to get every nice-looking woman he meets into his bed?"

Libby laughed. "Yes."

"Your mate is braver and more trusting than I thought."

"Kel isn't that bad. Besides, Nyssa is here too, so you don't have to worry."

"Oh, that makes me feel a whole lot better." Ricka laughed, her tone loaded with sarcasm. "I still think we should…" The room lights flickered. Wavy lines distorted her image and scrambled her words. Seconds later, the room dimmed and the screen went blank.

What the heck? Libby tapped several keys on the display panel, but nothing happened. Frustrated, she walked into the bedroom and swiped her hand over the sensor to activate the lights. When she still didn't get a response, she headed for the lower level. "Nyssa, any idea what's going on with the power?" she called as she descended the stairs.

She left the last step and froze, fear creeping up her spine. Boyd stood in the middle of the gathering room, aiming a laser weapon at Nyssa. The gun might not be as powerful as a repeater, but it could still cause some major injuries or even death.

Carl, the creep who always enjoyed grabbing her ass, stood next to him. His appearance hadn't changed much since the last time she'd seen him. His clothes were disheveled, and his stringy hair looked as if it hadn't seen a comb in days.

"Hello, again. Did you miss me?" Boyd asked.

She ignored his taunting sneer and moved closer to Nyssa. "Are you okay?" *Where the hell is Kel?* She secretly hoped they hadn't done anything to hurt him, and at the same time wished he'd show up soon to help them.

"I am fine." Nyssa nodded, never taking her angry glare off the two men.

"Why are you here?" Libby asked.

"You don't think I came all the way to this shitty planet for nothing, did you? I've come to collect my property."

"I am not *your* property." *Why can't the guy accept "no" for an answer?* "If you needed a bride so badly, why not handpick one from Earth? I'm sure your family could pay for whatever woman you wanted. Why bother with me?"

"I have no intention of marrying you, sweetheart. That was the story I used to get that hard-ass Ryos to turn you over to me."

"What are you talking about?" Libby asked.

"Contracting brides was my idea. It was a way to bring more women to Rivean." Boyd scratched his head. "Imagine how surprised I was when my uncle actually agreed to implement the program."

"I still don't understand. What does that have to do with me?"

"I'm selling you to the slavers."

Her chest muscles seized tight. She couldn't believe what she was hearing.

Boyd walked over to her. "Don't look so surprised. How do you think the Klorthons found you in that piece-of-shit bar in the first place?" Condescending arrogance dripped from his words. "Molock and I were working together. I located the women to sell, and he split the profits with me." He twirled a lock of her hair. "Blondes bring in a lot more money."

"You sick bastard." Libby slapped his hand away. "Your family is rich and powerful. Why would you need the money?"

Boyd ground his teeth. "My uncle is a greedy son of a bitch who believes everyone should earn their own way. The only reason he'd give me any money is if I paid it back with interest."

Libby had overheard plenty of miners complain about Dale Keagan's tightfisted and unethical business practices. She'd assumed his harsh treatment only applied to the employees, not his own family.

"Molock's contact wasn't happy about losing his shipment. If I don't deliver you, he's threatened to come after me." Boyd snickered. "And I like living too much to allow that to happen."

#

Damned spoiled female. Before Erak could take Libby home, Ryos had been informed of a problem with a visiting dignitary and asked him to stay behind and handle the situation. It wasn't so much a what as it was a who. The daughter of a visiting official refused to be escorted from her vessel by any of the guards. She'd insisted it had to be a hunter, more specifically, him.

Every time she arrived on Tarron, the female found a way to get him alone in her suite of rooms, or rather try to entice him into her bed. An invitation he'd never had any interest in and had always refused.

The hysterical outburst she'd thrown when he'd informed her he was now mated was neither pleasant nor amusing. He might not miss his parents, but sometimes them being who they were was useful. If they'd been home, he could have asked the commander to contact them and let them deal with her. Instead, he'd spent the remainder of the morning trying to placate the demanding female. He'd finally convinced her to let Ryos send another hunter to replace him. Preferably an unmated one.

He programmed the transport for his dwelling, his thoughts filled with getting back to Libby. He hated being separated from her, especially after the confrontation with Keagan. The vile man had been too eager to get his hands on her. His anxiety didn't lessen once he'd learned the colony's vessel hadn't departed as expected.

Kel had volunteered to escort Libby and his sister home, promising to remain until he returned. His friend might openly flirt with another male's mate, but Erak knew he could trust him not to touch her. Kel would protect her with his life.

The virtucom beeped, signaling an incoming transmission. He tapped the link, and Synge's image appeared on the screen. Concern etched the worry lines around his eyes. "Where are you?"

The urgency in his tone immediately made Erak wary. "On my way home. Why?"

"My mate was on a call with Libby, and the transmission ended abruptly. She tried to reconnect the link and did not have any luck. It might be nothing, but she was concerned. I am headed to your place now."

"I will meet you there." Before the call ended, Erak had accelerated the speed of the transport. He tried the links on the virtucom in his home and each of the personal communicators. All he got was interference. Even the tracker in the device he'd given Libby wasn't transmitting a signal.

#

Libby wished Boyd had mentioned the name of the contact. If she got out of this mess and could pass the information on to the hunters, it might help them capture the slavers and prevent any more women from being abducted.

Carl smacked Boyd's arm. "Grab her so we can go. We ain't got time for no small talk. The signal interrupter won't last forever. We need to be out of here before the power comes back on."

"It will be fine. Stop worrying."

"I'm not going anywhere with you," Libby said.

"I'm thinking you'll do as I say unless you want your new friend here to get hurt." Boyd grabbed her arm and shoved her toward the rear of the house.

"What should we do with this one?" Carl asked.

"Bring her along. We won't get as much money for her. Maybe they can sell her to one of the outlying pleasure ships, and we'll make up some of the money we lost from losing the other two."

By other two, Libby knew he meant Kala and Britta. She was fairly sure they were safely on their way back to Rivean.

"Yeah, or maybe he's got a buyer who's into ugly alien chicks." Carl grabbed Nyssa's arm and jerked her along with him.

"Get your hands off me, you sheraaat." She wrenched free of his grasp. "I can walk by myself."

"Fine, then start moving."

Libby couldn't believe this was happening. She'd known Boyd was dangerous, but she never imagined he'd be responsible for trafficking women. Now his life was in jeopardy and he was desperate, making him even more lethal. The communicator Erak had given her was still in her pocket. Once the interrupter stopped working, she might be able to get him a message. The only problem was how to do it without getting caught.

"This way." Boyd led them into the dense forest area to the left. Besides Nyssa's vehicle, Libby didn't see any signs of another transport. He must have approached the dwelling on foot.

"Let the females go." Kel moved out of the shadows. "Lower your weapons." He aimed his repeater at Carl's chest.

A man she'd never seen before stepped out from between two large trees. Before she could scream a warning, he pressed the end of his gun to Kel's head. "Not gonna happen," he said, an emotionless calm in his tone. The dark deadly glint in his eyes suggested the man wouldn't hesitate to shoot. "Hand it over." The man wrenched the repeater out of Kel's hand, then tucked it in the back of his pants.

"I figured there might be a problem. Good thing I had Asher wait outside." Boyd glared at Kel, then raised his weapon. "Too bad for you." The blast from the repeater made Libby jump.

Kel spun to the side, dropping face-first to the ground.

"No!" Nyssa screamed, trying to get to him.

Carl grabbed her around the waist, pinning Nyssa to his chest. "Leave him. There's nothing you can do for him now."

No, no, no. Libby glowered at Boyd and blinked back the tears. She refused to let the asshole see her cry. "You didn't have to shoot him. He wasn't a threat." She hated feeling helpless. Even without his weapon, they had a better chance of escape with Kel's help. There was nothing she could do now. If she tried anything, Boyd would follow through on his threat to hurt Nyssa.

"He probably overheard us talking and knows about my involvement with the slavers. I have too much at stake to risk him sharing the information with your boyfriend or the other hunters," Boyd said.

"You cold bastard, you could have brought him with us." Libby swiped the tear on her cheek.

"Didn't want to mess with it." He tipped his head at Asher. "Anything else we need to worry about?"

"Nah, we're good."

"Then let's get out of here before anyone else shows up."

#

By the time Erak reached his dwelling, he was frantic with worry. His imagination filled with every terrible scenario possible. Seeing Kel's transport parked by the side of his dwelling didn't minimize his stress. He'd barely exited his vehicle when Synge arrived.

"After we spoke, I tried to access the virtucom. I activated the tracker on Libby's personal communicator and could not get a location." Erak drew his weapon.

"You think the signal is being jammed somehow."

"It had occurred to me since we did not experience any interference."

"Hopefully, it is nothing." Synge slid the repeater from his holster.

Without another word, they headed for the front entrance. The sensor didn't activate, so he keyed in the emergency bypass to open the door. In case there was an actual threat, he didn't want to announce their presence. When they didn't find anyone, he silently signaled that he would search the upper level, leaving the lower area for Synge.

Erak met Synge back in the gathering room. "There is no one upstairs." He knew Kel would never take the females anywhere without notifying him first. Why hadn't he listened to his instincts? He never should have left Libby's side, not until he was sure Boyd was off the planet. If something happened to her, it would be his fault.

"Nothing here either. No signs of a struggle." Synge glanced toward the rear exit. "Could they be somewhere else on your property?"

"Doubtful." Erak ran his hand through his hair. "We are wasting time."

Synge clapped a hand on his shoulder. "I know you want to find her, but we need to be thorough. We will do a quick check out back, then contact the commander with an update."

Knowing his friend was right didn't help the pressure bearing down on his chest. Giving him a quick nod, he headed outside.

They hadn't gone far before he spotted Kel's unmoving form lying on the ground next to a group of tall trees. *Fuck, please do not let him be dead.* "I found Kel," Erak hollered, holstering his weapon and rushing over to his friend. He crouched beside him, slowly easing him onto his back. The left shoulder area of his shirt was soaked with blood. His forehead bled from a jagged gash.

"Is he still alive?" Synge moved to his other side, warily observing their surroundings.

"Of course, I am still alive," Kel snarled, his eyes fluttering open. "That idiot shoots worse than my mother. It will take more than one of those human toys to end my life."

"I am glad you live, but where is my mate?"

"Keagan took her and Nyssa." Kel propped up on his elbows, trying to sit up. "I am sorry, my friend. I failed you."

"Do not apologize. You nearly gave your life to protect them." Erak braced an arm behind his injured shoulder. "Help me get him to his feet."

"Was he alone?" Synge asked.

"No. There were two others with him, both human."

Synge holstered his weapon and leaned forward to grab Kel's other arm. "How did you manage to get shot?"

"I was checking on the power displays when they arrived. I only saw one other male enter the house with him. I did not know the other one was out here; otherwise he never would have been able to disarm me." Kel staggered a couple of steps. "Before I was shot, I overheard them say they were headed back to their ship. They are not returning to Rivean. Keagan was working with Molock and plans to sell the females to the slavers."

"Then we need to stop them before they get off the planet," Erak said.

"Come, we need to get you to a medical unit. We can contact the commander on the way," Synge said.

"I can use the med kit in the transport. If you are going after them, I am coming with you. I intend to make the sheraaat pay for his poor aim," Kel said.

"You can have whatever is left of him after I make him suffer for touching my mate."

"Agreed."

His friend was going to be very disappointed, because if Boyd had done anything to hurt the two females he cared about, he planned to make sure he suffered. A lot.

CHAPTER TWELVE

Libby sat in the rear seat of the transport with Asher on her left and Nyssa on her right. The man hadn't spoken a word since they'd left Erak's house, and being this close to him made her skin crawl.

Light from the mid-afternoon rays ensured good visibility. She had a clear view of the long line of transports waiting to access the hunter command facility. It meant they would be delayed from leaving the planet, and she didn't regret feeling good about it.

Carl maneuvered their vehicle off the main road and parked in a secluded spot. "Great plan. I told you letting Asher kill those guards was a mistake." He banged his fist on the control panel. "The entire place is locked down, and they're searching vehicles. There's no way we'll be able to get to the ship now."

"Shut up and calm down," Boyd ordered. "You heard them, they were instructed not to leave until we launched. Getting rid of them was necessary." He jerked his thumb toward Libby. "We need her, or we don't get paid."

"Without a ship, it's gonna be a little hard to deliver. How the fuck do you plan to get off the planet?" Carl gripped the side of his seat until his knuckles whitened.

"There has to be another place where we can hire a ship." Boyd turned sideways in his seat so he faced Nyssa. "I'll bet you know of one, don't you?"

Nyssa stubbornly crossed her arms and glared at him. "What makes you think I would help you even if I did?"

"Because if you don't Asher is gonna start using his knife on her." Boyd's menacing gaze flashed to Libby.

"I thought you said she was worth a lot of money. I am sure the slavers will not pay you if she is dead."

"I didn't say he was going to kill her. Only make her bleed some. There're plenty of places he can cut her where it'll hurt like hell but won't kill her. Trust me when I tell you my associate knows every one of them."

Asher rolled on his hip and dug a thin silver object out of his pocket. He pressed a tab on the side, and a thin, sharp-looking blade flipped out, locking into place. For added effect, he held Libby's wrist against his thigh and laid the shiny surface flat against the underside of her arm.

Libby gasped and didn't move, afraid if she spoke, he'd use it as an excuse to start slicing. Carl widened his eyes and swiped his tongue back and forth across his lower lip as if anticipating a possible bloodletting.

"It would be a shame to cover her beautiful body with a bunch of scars." Boyd's harsh voice pitched higher. "Now, tell me where to find a ship so we can get off this fucking planet."

#

Erak sat in the pilot's seat of his transport and engaged the virtucom link. An image of the commander materialized on the screen.

"Any news?" Ryos asked.

He knew Synge had contacted the commander before heading to his home to inform him there might be a problem. "Keagan has taken my mate and sister. Kel was shot."

"Inconvenient flesh wound," Kel grumbled. He had his back to Erak and had perched his ass on the edge of the adjacent seat with his long legs hanging out of the vehicle, anchoring him to the ground. Synge stood on the other side of him, examining his injured shoulder.

"There were three of them. We assume they will be heading back to their ship," Erak said.

Ryos shook his head. "They will not be able to reach it. The guards who escorted Keagan were found dead. I have locked down the facility."

The news was good and bad. Good because it prevented the males from taking Erak's family off planet. Bad because they now had no way to locate them.

"We will find them." The commander's hardened gaze passed between them. "I will contact you if I learn anything else."

"Yes, sir." Erak stared at the blank screen. Was he supposed to sit here and wait? He fisted his hands to keep from hitting something, anything to relieve the helplessness washing through him. He got out of the vehicle and walked around to stand next to his friends.

Synge swiped Kel's wound with an antiseptic cleanser. "We need to think about this logically," Kel said. "If Keagan plans to sell the females, then he will want to find another way off the planet. The bazaar is the only place close enough where he might be able to access another vessel."

"How would he know about the bazaar, or even how to find it? I do not believe he has ever been on Tarron before. Tracking my mate from the facility is one thing, but knowing where to find alternative transportation is more difficult," Erak said.

Synge applied a thick layer of sealing gel over Kel's wound. "Dammit, take it easy with that stuff." Kel winced and gripped the door frame. "He would not, but Nyssa would."

"How does she...did you take her there?" Erak asked.

"Maybe a time or two."

"You took advantage of my sister?"

"No. It is not what you are thinking, so stop looking at me like that." Kel gave Synge a pleading glance. "Talk some sense into him, will you?"

Synge shook his head. "You do have a reputation with the females, and all the teasing does not help." He slipped the med kit into a storage compartment under the rear seat.

"Nyssa is like a sister to me. I would never try to take advantage of her." Kel rolled his shoulder. "She is a lot smarter than you will admit, and asked me to go along as an escort. Nothing more."

"As much as I would enjoy seeing you take a swing at him for all the times he has flirted with my mate, he is correct. If these men are desperate, they may force your sister to help them find another ship. It is a reasonable assumption," Synge said.

"I do not want to drive around based on a guess. What if you are wrong and we waste valuable time trying to find them?"

"Maybe we won't. Did you deactivate the tracker on your mate's communicator after we arrived?" Synge asked.

"No, why?"

Synge pointed at a small flashing light on the device attached to the side of Erak's belt. "It appears to be active."

#

Once Nyssa gave them directions to the bazaar, Asher tucked the knife in his pocket. Libby tucked her arm closer to her body. She rubbed her wrist, trying to remove the faint impression and erase the horrible memory of having the blade pressed against her skin.

"Which way?" Carl drove through a large area filled with transports.

"The landing site is straight ahead, behind the market," Nyssa said.

He drove past the pad designated for visitors and lined with a wide variety of ships and shuttles.

"Stop here," Boyd said. As soon as they stopped, he glanced over his shoulder at Asher. "Find someone to get us the hell out of here."

Asher grunted, then slipped out and headed toward the pads.

The silence and tension in the cramped vehicle frayed Libby's nerves. She kept telling herself the waiting was a good thing. The longer it took Asher to find a vessel, the more time it gave Erak to find them.

Carl pointed out the front view pane. "That didn't take long."

Libby leaned to the left and spotted Asher heading back in their direction, accompanied by a Tarron. The man towered at least five inches over the human male's six-foot height. His entire outfit was black, made of a fabric resembling leather, and reminded Libby of the bikers she'd seen back on Earth.

Boyd got out, then turned around to glare at them. "You two stay put and keep your mouths shut. I'm sure I don't need to tell you what will happen if you don't."

Carl opened his door and only made it two steps before Boyd said, "You stay here. Make sure they don't try anything."

"Fine." He didn't bother to get back inside. Once Boyd was out of earshot, Carl muttered, "I didn't sign up to be a fucking babysitter."

Libby assumed the stranger had a ship their captors planned to procure. She couldn't hear the men's conversation, but by Asher's angry expression, she didn't think the negotiations were going well. Carl braced his arms on the door frame and nervously rocked back and forth, his attention seemingly focused on the argument. Periodically, he tipped his head and glanced in their direction.

"I am so sorry for bringing them here, but I could not let them hurt you," Nyssa whispered.

"This is not your fault. I would have done the same thing for you." Libby squeezed her hand.

"My brother will come for us, I know it." Nyssa placed a hand on her arm. "He would die before he lets anything happen to his true mate."

True mate. Libby still couldn't believe they'd been destined to be together. Now that she'd found him, she was going to do everything in her power not to lose him. The hunters were probably watching Boyd's ship, and wouldn't know to look for them here. Right now, her biggest problem was finding a way to let Erak know where they were.

She brushed her hand along the fabric of her pants, feeling the communication device hidden in her pocket. If only she could find a way to activate it without being seen by their abductors.

Boyd returned and slapped the top of the transport. "Get them out." The men must have come to an agreement, because Asher and the stranger disappeared between two shuttles.

"You heard him, let's go." Carl opened the rear door and waited for them to get out. Libby was glad to be out of the overly warm and confining vehicle. She took a moment to stretch her legs and used the opportunity to look around without detection. The area was vacant. Not a single person in sight, dashing her hopes of attracting any help.

She decided it was probably for the best since Boyd had demonstrated that he didn't have a problem killing someone.

Nyssa must have sensed what she was thinking. "We will find another way."

"Hey, no talking." Carl retrieved his weapon, then motioned

with it for them to follow Boyd.

When they reached the rear of a medium-sized ship, Boyd stopped. Asher had taken a position several feet away. He maintained a soldier's stance, his gaze alert and focused on their surroundings. Libby wondered if he'd had some kind of military training.

"How soon can we leave?" Boyd asked the Tarron.

The stranger, who'd been facing away from them, turned. His gaze focused on Nyssa, then moved to her. He glowered and removed his hand from an exterior sensor panel. The sound of grinding metal filled the air and the partially lowered cargo bay ramp slammed to a stop. "The agreement was for transportation back to Rivean for the three of you. There was no mention of any females." His hand slid to the weapon holstered on his hip. "I am afraid the price we discussed will now have to be doubled."

"You can't do that. We had a deal," Boyd snarled.

"Deals can always be renegotiated." His attention strayed to Libby, slowly inspecting every inch of her body. He took a couple of steps forward. His large frame hovered much too close. With Carl standing right behind her she had nowhere to go.

She cringed when he slid his fingers through her hair, then lifted some strands to his nose, and sniffed. "You can keep your rivets. I will take this female in exchange for safe passage."

Libby swallowed hard against the bile threatening to rise. She resisted the urge to slap him. Instead, she fisted her hands so tightly her nails dug into her palms. Surely they weren't going to let him take her. Not that she wanted to go with Boyd and his crew either, but right now, she preferred them over this menacing giant.

Asher emerged on the other side of Carl with his gun drawn.

"The woman has been promised to another and is not for sale." Boyd gave Nyssa a shove. "I will give you this female instead."

"I do not care about your previous arrangement. You will give me her, or there is no deal." The Tarron drew his weapon and yanked Libby in front of him.

No, no, no. She screamed and clawed at the arm encircling her throat.

"Be still." He tightened his grip, keeping her back firmly lodged against his chest and constricting the flow of air to her lungs.

Her vision faltered, and she gasped. She couldn't afford to black out. What would stop him from simply tossing her over his shoulder and carrying her off? No way was she going to make it easy for him to get her on his ship.

She stopped struggling but continued to cling to his arm. He loosened his grip enough for her to gulp air back into her burning lungs. "Better yet, I will take the female, and you will find someone else to help you," the Tarron said.

Libby stared at the weapons aimed in her direction and hoped like hell the man using her as a shield didn't do something stupid to get her shot.

#

"I told you this is where they would go." Kel hooked the belt containing the holster and repeater Erak had loaned him around his waist.

"Stop gloating. I am still not happy about you bringing my sister here in the first place." His friend's goading was the only thing keeping Erak from going crazy at the moment. The thought of anything happening to Libby was killing him. Ever since he found out she'd been taken, he'd beaten himself up with guilt.

He should have refused the commander's request to handle the issue with the official's daughter and stayed with his mate. If he had, she'd be safe now. *Or, you might be dead.* Synge's earlier words echoed through his thoughts.

Using the system in his transport, the three men had tracked the signal from Libby's communication device to the bazaar. They left the transport parked far enough away from the visiting ships to keep from being noticed. Once they left the vehicle, Erak switched the information over to his handheld unit. The signal was growing stronger, indicating she was somewhere near the designated landing pads on the outskirts of the large outdoor market.

From the indicator on the screen, his mate had not been taken off the planet. A fact that could change at any moment. He wouldn't relax until he knew both females were safe and unharmed.

Erak glanced at the device again. "If this is correct, we are very close." He pointed. "They should be that direction."

"Let us go get your mate. I will take the right." Kel headed into the dense forest area bordering the perimeter of the property.

"I have the other side." Synge retrieved his own weapon

before sprinting off to the left, leaving him to take a direct approach.

Erak quickened his pace, driven by the overpowering desire to find and protect the woman he loved. Breaking through the edge of trees, he hesitated briefly to search for signs of movement before moving toward the rear of a shuttle. He caught sight of Kel and Synge stealthily taking similar positions farther away on both sides of him. The sound of males arguing caught his attention. Raising his repeater, he slowly eased his way along the side of the vessel.

A Tarron male had one arm wrapped around Libby's neck and a laser weapon in the other pointed at Boyd's head. "I am keeping the female." He dragged her backward toward a ship with its loading ramp partially dropped. Other than her fearful expression, she appeared to be unharmed.

He was thankful she was alive, but it didn't keep him from wanting to rip the male's head off for daring to touch his mate. Erak took a calming breath and suppressed the roar fighting to burst from his lungs. He wouldn't be any good to her if he lost control of his temper. Quietly, he eased toward them, mentally noting the details of the situation.

The two men Kel had mentioned stood on either side of Boyd, their weapons aimed at the male holding Libby. The one farthest away from him gripped his sister's arm. "What the hell do we do now?" The man nervously glanced from the Tarron to Boyd.

If the argument escalated any further or one of the males lost control, Libby was in the direct line of fire, and could be killed. Erak wasn't prepared to take the risk. He stepped into the open, drawing everyone's attention. "You will lower your weapons and release the females."

"Ah, the so-called boyfriend," Boyd spouted arrogantly. "Do you really think you can take on all of us and survive?"

"Not by myself, no. With their help, yes." Erak cocked his head to the side, enjoying their equally surprised expressions when they saw Synge and Kel move into positions and surround them.

Boyd stared at Kel. "You...I shot you. You should be dead."

"Not with that tiny piece of metal you call a weapon." Kel snorted and aimed his repeater at Carl. "Nyssa, I need you to move away from him."

"Gladly." She yanked her arm out of the male's grasp, then grabbed his gun. She stepped back, then aimed it at his chest.

"Toss your weapons, then get down on your knees with your hands behind your heads," Kel said.

One by one, the three males did as he'd ordered.

With the majority of the threat minimized, Erak moved forward, keeping his weapon aimed at the male holding Libby. "Release my mate."

#

When he'd first arrived, Erak's gaze had briefly held hers, and she'd glimpsed his love through the controlled anger in his expression. Libby had no idea how he'd found them, and right now, she didn't care. All that mattered was that he was here.

"Find another female, hunter. I plan to keep this one," said the male behind her. He lifted his free elbow and pressed the panel on the side of the ship. Gears ground into action, and the ramp began the remainder of its descent.

Oh my God. Was the asshole really going to drag her into the vessel? With her pinned to his chest like a shield, none of the men would be able to fire. Not without hitting her. She needed to do something to help them, because there was no way she was going to let him take her anywhere.

"Shoot!" she screamed, then bit into his arm as hard as she could. Next, using the move Nyssa taught her during training practice, she elbowed him in the ribs, then brought her foot down hard on top of his. He snarled, loosening his grip enough for her to slip beneath his arm. She quickly dove to the side and hit the ground on her hands and knees.

She heard a shot fire and looked over her shoulder. The Tarron had taken a hit in the chest and fallen backward. The top half of his body was sprawled on the lower portion of the metal ramp.

"Are you all right?" Erak gently helped her off the ground. "Are you hurt?" He ran his hands along her arms, eying her from top to bottom before pulling her into his arms and kissing her forehead. "I thought I had lost you. I am so sorry I did not stay with you."

"I'm fine, and don't you dare blame yourself for this. They would have tried to kill you like they did Kel." The thought had crossed her mind more times than she wanted to admit, and she'd been thankful he hadn't been at their home when Boyd arrived. She pressed her head against his chest, breathing in his scent, refusing to let go.

A few seconds later, Nyssa had her arms wrapped around both of them. "I knew you would come. How did you find us?"

"The communication device I gave my mate has a tracker." Erak clutched Libby as if she might vanish if he let her go.

Nyssa frowned. "You kept track of her as if she were a pet?"

"No, I…" he muttered.

"As far as I'm concerned, it was the best gift ever." Libby kissed him on the chin.

Kel walked up beside Nyssa and draped his arm across her shoulder. "How are you doing?"

"You want to know how I'm doing? Let me show you." She shrugged away from him, then punched him hard in his good shoulder.

He caught her wrist before she could hit him again. "What was that for?"

"For letting me think you were dead. Do not ever do that again, do you hear me?"

Kel chuckled. "I promise."

Synge strolled up to the group. "The commander is sending a team to collect Keagan and his friends. They should be here shortly."

"Come with me." Nyssa took Kel's hand and led him to where the three men were kneeling on the ground. Their hands were now cuffed behind their backs. "Can you help this one up?" She pointed at Carl.

"Sure." Kel grabbed his arm and hoisted him to his feet.

"Here is what I think of your 'ugly alien chick' comment." She raised her leg and kneed him in the groin.

He groaned, doubled over, and dropped back on his knees.

She grinned at Kel mischievously.

"Do not look at me like that." He covered the front of his pants and almost tripped trying to get away from her. "I already said I promise."

"Just making sure."

Libby watched the interaction between the two and laughed. She stayed snuggled against Erak's chest and had no interest in moving any time soon.

Synge's communicator beeped. He unclipped it from his belt

and held it to his ear, listening to whoever was speaking. "Yes, they are fine." He smiled at Libby.

"I think she will have to call you later." Synge paused, then winked. "It may take some time before her mate releases her."

Synge's good humor faded, and he held his communicator out to Libby. "Please speak to my mate. I am in jeopardy of losing male parts if you do not."

"We can't have that now, can we?" Erak released her so she could take the device but refused to let go of her other hand.

"Hey," Libby said.

"Please tell me someone shot that son of a bitch."

"Sorry, no." Libby would have done it herself if she'd been able to. Maybe not kill him, but after all he'd put them through, wound him, definitely.

"That's too bad," Ricka said. "Are you going to be okay? Do you need anything?"

She glanced at Erak. "I have everything I need."

"If you're sure."

"Positive."

"Promise me you'll call me later," Ricka said.

"I will." She disconnected the link and handed the device back to Synge. "I think your parts are safe now."

He grinned. "I am forever in your debt."

It didn't take long for the commander's transport to arrive. The vehicle was a larger model with a cargo area built into the rear. Several hunters, including Ryos, got out. He approached their group with purposeful strides. "I am happy to see you are both unharmed." He regarded Nyssa, then her.

"Thank you." She glanced at Kel and Synge, who'd joined the other two hunters and were dragging the prisoners to their feet.

"You better be here to take me home. My uncle will have your head," Boyd shouted.

"What will happen to him? You won't be sending him back to Rivean, will you?" If they turned him over to the colony patrol, there was a good chance his uncle would have him released. Libby shivered, knowing he'd be able to do this to more women, or find a way to come after her again.

"He will be going to Drichtarr. Even Dale Keagan is not powerful enough to have someone removed from that facility," Ryos said.

Libby relaxed a little, hearing the news. She'd heard about the desolate planet that housed one of the worse prisons in the quadrant.

"It is much better than he deserves, though his life will not be worth much once the other inhabitants learn about his involvement with enslaving females," Erak said.

"I think it might be best if you took several days off from your duties. I assume you would like to spend some time with your mate."

Erak gave her one of his rare smiles. "I cannot think of anything I would rather do more."

Ryos turned his attention to Nyssa. "I know you have not finished your training, but if you are interested, I would like to have you work as escort for visiting dignitaries."

"That would be seriously awesome."

"Nyssa," Erak groaned, pinching the bridge of his nose.

His sister grinned. "I mean yes, I would be happy to help."

Ryos appeared to be amused. "Good. Stop by my office tomorrow, and we will discuss it further."

"Would you like to go home now?" Erak asked and scooped Libby into his arms.

Libby wrapped her arms around his neck. "Yes, please." *More than anything.*

CHAPTER THIRTEEN

"It is not much farther to the pool." Erak's anxious tone seemed to match the racing beat of her heart.

Libby stared out the view pane of the transport. It amazed her how easily Erak maneuvered the narrow roadway only slightly wider than their vehicle. The tall trees and abundant plant life on either side were so close, she could touch them.

It was hard not to think about everything that had happened in the short time since she'd been abducted by Boyd. She'd spent two wonderful days alone with Erak, the majority of it in bed making love or nestled in his arms. He'd kept her so busy, she rarely had time to think about how close they'd come to losing each other.

Then there had been the surprise communication from his parents via the virtucom link. Though the older couple had kept the conversation, more like interrogation, brief, she was relieved when it was over. The claiming with their son had happened so quickly, Libby had expected them to be upset by the news. She'd been shocked to learn they were thrilled he had mated a human, seeing it as an opportunity for improved negotiations with Rivean and Earth. The fact that Dale Keagan's nephew had been involved in the abductions seemed to impress them even more.

After the call ended, she understood why Erak had seemed so closed off with his emotions, and why he had such an aversion to dealing with anyone in the political world. Libby had a feeling he'd been afraid she might change her mind about joining after meeting them. He'd offered her numerous assurances that they would have limited interactions with those two members of his family. Something she'd found to be completely adorable.

Nyssa had arrived earlier in the day and given her a gown for the ceremony. The fabric had a soft, satiny feel and shimmered a translucent gold. It fit her perfectly, clinging to her body as if it had been specially designed for her. The sheer material left nothing to the imagination, and she suspected it was the reason Erak's sister had picked it out for her. Thankfully, she'd also provided Libby with a smock-like gown made of a thicker material to wear over it.

Libby was glad the ritual included only the two of them. She would have died of embarrassment if she'd had to stand in front of a group of people wearing the outfit.

The road widened, and Erak stopped the transport. "We will have to walk from here." He reached behind her seat to grab a large pack, then got out and walked around to help her out.

"Is it far?" Libby inspected the sandals on her feet. She wasn't dressed to go traipsing through a jungle.

He slung the strap of the bag over his shoulder. "No." He grinned, then scooped her into his arms and started walking. "I believe this is part of your Earth custom."

Locking her arms around his neck, she pressed a kiss to his cheek. "It is, thank you." She didn't have the heart to tell him the tradition involved a doorway.

They hadn't gone far before they entered a secluded clearing. "This is where we will say our vows." Erak lowered her to the ground.

She made a slow circle, committing every detail of the place to memory. The ground was covered with the same unusually soft yellow grass she'd seen the day Nyssa had taken her shopping. A waterfall at least ten feet tall splashed down over large boulders into a shallow pool containing water the color of dark amethyst. "This is unbelievably incredible."

"I am glad you like it." Erak set the pack on the ground, then retrieved two large towels and a blanket. He set the towels next to the pool and unfolded the blanket, spreading it out on the grass.

"What is that for?" Libby didn't remember anything about a blanket in the ceremony.

"Later." He presented her with one of those rare smiles she loved.

#

Erak saw desire spark in her gaze, and heat surged through him. There was nothing he wanted more than to bond with Libby and feel her writhing underneath him as he slowly possessed her. "Are you ready?"

"Yes."

"You must be certain. This is not like a human marriage. The words we speak will bind us together forever. I could not bear..." Old insecurities rushed through him. It would destroy him if she changed her mind and rejected him after they entered the waters.

She placed her hands on his cheeks. "I love you. I have never been more certain of anything in my life."

He drew her into his arms and into a kiss. He greedily tasted, taunted, claimed. She belonged to him, and he was about to make her his permanently.

By the time he released her, they were both panting heavily. "If we do not stop now, I fear we will not make it into the pool."

"Then show me what we need to do." Libby unhooked the clasp on her smock. She pushed it off her shoulders, letting it fall to the ground. The lustrous golden material of the gown she wore was nearly transparent. It clung to her form, outlining every enticing curve, and he took his time perusing every inch of her. Even the sacred waters weren't going to cool the fire tearing through him or lessen his hardening erection.

"After we remove each other's clothing, we will enter the pool and recite our bonding vows." He wasn't worried Libby wouldn't know what to do. Nyssa had already coached her on what she needed to say. He ran the back of his hand along the exposed skin of her chest before undoing the single fastener between her breasts. Pushing the fabric aside, he skimmed her nipples with his thumbs, causing her to shudder.

"So beautiful." He slid the fabric over her shoulders and down her arms slowly until the gown joined the smock on the ground. He lowered his arms to his sides and waited for Libby. "Now you."

Grabbing the hem of his shirt, she pushed it up along his chest. Erak leaned forward, making it easier for her to slip it over his head. She ran her hands down his chest, grazing his skin with her nails.

Her expression hinted at mischief, and he knew she wasn't done torturing him. After undoing his zipper, she ran her fingers along his shaft at the same time she removed his pants. He forced back a groan and had to fist his hands against his thighs to keep from touching her. "Be warned, I am going to make you pay for that later."

She swiped the tip of her tongue across her lower lip and giggled. "Promise?"

Growling, he took her hand and led her to the edge of the pool. He lifted her around the waist and waded through the water until it touched his abdomen before setting her on her feet. He held her ice-blue gaze and placed his right hand against her cheek. "I share with you the bond of a mate. Truer than true. Joined together forever and always."

Libby smiled, then cupped his cheek and repeated the words back to him.

As if in approval of their solemn vows, the waters darkened and ripples ran across its transparent surface. Erak never understood how or why the waters reacted the way they did, and he didn't care. The only thing that mattered was Libby. She was his true mate, and they were officially joined.

"That was kind of amazing. Does it mean we're bonded now?" Libby asked.

"Yes, you belong to me, and I will never let you go."

"Good thing, because I hadn't planned on letting you go either."

"I love you, my mate." He grabbed her ass and hoisted her out of the water.

"What are you doing?" she squealed, wrapping her legs around his waist.

"I believe I have a promise to keep." He turned and headed for the edge of the pool, looking forward to claiming her all over again.

EPILOGUE

"Congratulations on your recent joining. How is your female adjusting to her new life after her ordeal?" Ryos envied his junior officer's happiness in finding his true mate.

Erak entered the office and took a seat in the chair opposite the control display. "She is doing fine, thank you for asking."

"Your sister is doing well escorting visiting emissaries. If you have no objections, I am going to give her the tasks permanently. I have other assignments here in the city better suited to your talents," Ryos said. The new duties would also ensure that Erak remained closer to his mate. After everything the female had been through, it was the least he could do for the couple.

"I am sure she will appreciate the opportunity," Erak said.

"The main reason I wanted to see you was because I have received some information that may help us find Larn and Balok."

"What have you discovered?" Erak didn't seem impressed.

Ryos understood his lack of emotion. This was not the first bit of news they'd received in the last few months. So far, none of the leads had been useful. If the members of his team were still alive, the hunters were no closer to finding them. "Our source confirmed someone from Ryserna contracted Molock to detain your ship," Ryos said.

Erak leaned forward, showing more interest. "Do you have any idea who?"

Ryos had always wondered how the Klorthons were able to attack the ship so soon after he'd ordered them to find the missing females. Erak had informed him about the warrior's discussion concerning his selection to be sold as a breeder. At the time, Ryos hadn't given it much thought. Now it made sense. Members of his team were being targeted specifically. Whoever sent the warriors after his men was also responsible for Larn and Balok being sold to the fighting arena.

Ryos rubbed his chin. "Nothing yet?"

"Do you think our trip to the planet had anything to do with it?"

He knew Erak and his team hadn't spent more than a day on Ryserna after escorting the emissary's daughter. Certainly not enough time to create any enemies. "We do not know."

"Any chance this person is providing false information to keep us from finding them?" Erak asked.

Ryos shook his head. "We have no reason to doubt this new lead. The information comes from a reliable contact."

"How long before we have an answer?"

"It may take several weeks. I am sorry I do not have better news. I know you were close to your team." Ryos got to his feet. "There is nothing anyone can do until we get word. Please express my good wishes to your mate."

"Thank you, sir. I will."

Once he was alone, Ryos returned to his seat. He tapped a key on the panel to bring the information he'd recently received on the screen. After scrolling through the limited data, he stopped and brought up an image. An image of a male he'd known for years and trusted with his life. Shortly after he'd received the communication, the new team had found his friend in a deserted building, his body badly beaten.

He stared at the picture and ran his fingertip along the scar that ran from his right cheekbone to his jaw. There were very few people from his past he'd considered friends. The male in the image with his throat slashed had been one of them.

Ryos had no doubt the information he'd received was accurate, or that they were getting closer to the truth. He wouldn't stop searching until he found those responsible. And when he did, he'd make them pay for their treachery.

Also by Nola Robertson

Tarron Hunter Series

Hunter Claimed
Hunter Enslaved
Hunter Unchained
Hunter Forbidden
Hunter Scorned
Hunter Avenged

ABOUT THE AUTHOR

Nola Robertson grew up in the Midwest and eventually migrated to a rural town in New Mexico, where she lives with her husband and three cats, all with unique personalities and a lot of attitude.

Though she started her author career writing paranormal and sci-fi romance, it didn't take long for her love of solving mysteries to have her writing cozies. When she's not busy working on her next DIY project or reading, she's plotting her next mystery adventure.

Printed in Dunstable, United Kingdom

64082109R00077